IT'S ABOUT UNDERSTANDING, ACCEPTANCE AND MOST OF ALL—LOVE...

"This book, partly a series of vignettes about parents of Gay people, is their story, but it is also my story— how I started my work and where I am now: initiating and conducting workshops for families of Gay people at New York area Y's. In view of the toll the dread AIDS epidemic has taken on the already shaky Gay image; the families who ache over losing contact with their Gay sons or daughters; the hoopla and hype of current literature, films and theater, I believe it is timely and fitting for troubled families of Gay people to acquire some savvy from others who have grappled with accepting—and loving—their Gay children as the Gay people they really are. And then, perhaps, in the not-too-distant future, the Gay child will not have to ask, 'Are you still my mother?' Or—'Are you still my family?'"

—from *Are You Still My Mother?*

"Gloria Back has given parents of homosexual children hope which, in the emotional turmoil that inevitably accompanies the discovery that a child is gay, can seem lost to them forever. The wonderful workshops the author has established clear the path to understanding and acceptance of a homosexual son or daughter and help ease the pain of adjustment to this new and unfamiliar factor in their lives."

—"Dear Meg" Whitcomb

Are You Still My Mother?

Are You Still My Family?

Gloria Guss Back

WARNER BOOKS

A Warner Communications Company

Copyright © 1985 by Gloria Guss Back
All rights reserved.

Warner Books, Inc., 75 Rockefeller Plaza, New York, NY 10019

 A Warner Communications Company

Printed in the United States of America
First Printing: September 1985
10 9 8 7 6 5 4 3 2 1

Book design: H. Roberts Design

Library of Congress Cataloging in Publication Data

Back, Gloria Guss.
     Are you still my mother?

     Bibliography: p. 235
     1. Homosexuals—United States—Family relationships.
2. Parent and child—United States. 3. Interpersonal
relations. I. Title.
HQ76.3.U5B32   1985   306.8'74   85-7152
ISBN 0-446-38195-0 (U.S.A.) (pbk.)
          0-446-38196-9 (Canada) (pbk.)

To Gene, for his unblinking,
unwavering support of me and mine,
and to my son, Jeff

Contents

Acknowledgments

Thank you, Kenny and Sam, for your thoughts, feelings and for giving this book the once-over at least thrice.

Thank you, Sue Nirenberg: your sense of organization, optimism and enthusiasm provided me with invaluable assistance. (Besides, you were fun.)

I am ever grateful to Mario Sartori for his belief in the importance of what I have to say.

Introduction

After Kenny, my younger son, told me he was Gay, I spent years trying to understand my reactions: the blow to my ego, the hurt, the bewilderment, the confusion. During those years of struggle while I tried to learn, to understand and to come to grips with what it means to be a homosexual, to be the parent of a homosexual and to be homophobic ("an irrational revulsion to homosexuals"), I searched in vain for other parents in my situation. I needed to share my feelings, but I also knew *how* I wanted to share. I wanted to find a small, intimate group which met weekly to be led by a trained therapist, knowledgeable about homosexuality, who would listen to, guide and field questions from dismayed, guilt-ridden, puzzled parents like me.

Although I pored over the various community, family service and mental health organization catalogs (noting how they touched more and more on the most intimate human problems), I didn't find a single class, workshop or group such as the one I envisioned. I pondered. If as much as 10 percent of the population was Gay (as statistics show), then there must be millions who had a Gay family member. But where were they? Weren't there others who wanted to connect with family members under professional guidance? Was I the only parent who found it difficult to adjust to having a Gay child? Had these other parents of Gays no need or desire for the learning and sharing I so deeply wanted? Impossible. I felt sure there were many other parents like me, frustrated in their need to find each other—parents in search of a place where they could meet under the auspices of a respected and recognized institution.

But as time passed and I had once again enrolled in college as a mature adult determined to finish with a bona fide degree (even if I had to fight senility), the nagging feeling persisted that there must be other parents of Gays who needed to exchange thoughts and feelings. Then, one day when I was given an open-topic research assignment, a light bulb lit up in my head. Here was an opportunity to ferret out other parents of Gays and to discuss our mutual problem.

This would be my research topic. I would invade the privacy of varying and disparate parents of Gay people. We would share one huge crying towel. We would give vent to our feelings of hurt, anger and prejudice. But through our give-and-take we would wade through it all triumphant. We would arrive at a positive understanding of our children. And so it was that I embarked on the journey that became the genesis of this book.

Of course, I was brought up short. My fantasies about such happy endings were, more often than not, just fantasies. But still, I learned from these parents; I learned from those who adapted in some degree to a Gay son or daughter; and I learned from those who could not or would not adapt at all.

I was able to contact over sixty-five parents of Gay people by means of a questionnaire, letters, calls, interviews, and directly, meeting with them privately or in the the workshops I (now a graduate social worker) lead myself. I also talked to some Gay sons and daughters about how their families reacted to their "coming out." Many parents who responded had had a workable, if not loving, relationship with their children until their child disclosed his/her Gay orientation ("coming out"), then the relationship deteriorated. Shaken by their perception of homosexuality as a calamity, feeling helpless and bewildered, some parents turned to parents of Gays self-help groups; some to private therapy; some, like me, searched in vain for professionally led small workshops. Others just brooded but did nothing. The parents who reacted violently—even brutally—to their Gay sons and daughters, with rare exceptions, lost them.

This book, partly a series of vignettes about parents of Gay people, is their story, but it is also my story—how I started my work and where I am now: initiating and conducting workshops for families of Gay people at New York area Y's. In view of the effect the dread AIDS epidemic has had on the already shaky Gay image; the growing number of families who ache over losing contact with their Gay sons or daughters; and the hoopla and hype of current literature, films and theater, I believe it is timely and fitting for troubled families of Gay people to acquire some savvy from others who have grappled with accepting—and loving—their Gay children as the Gay people they really are. And then, perhaps, in the not-too-distant future, the Gay child will not have to ask, "Are you still my mother?" or "Are you still my family?"

My Story

...The same sweet smile, the same sad tears
The cries at night, the nightmare fears
Sons of the brave, or sons unknown
All were children like your own
So long ago, so long ago
Sons of tycoons or sons of the farms
All of the children ran from your arms
Through fields of gold, through fields of ruin
All of the children vanish too soon....

—Jacques Brel is Alive and Well
and Living in Paris

KENNY'S DISCLOSURE

I can hardly believe the change in me. . . .

About fourteen years ago, I was a somewhat conventional widow living in Forest Hills, New York, with two college-student sons, Jeff and Kenny. My husband Fred had died of leukemia two years earlier, and I tried to exercise a modicum of control at home. Dealing with two male rebels who delighted in testing me was not easy. I tried to set limits: a violation of those limits would be girls in the house unless I was home, earsplitting music on the stereo at 3 A.M., friends coming and going at all hours, hamburgers sizzling in the skillet at 2 A.M. Kenny and Jeff, basking in the newness of being the only men in the house, flexed their muscles and bucked me at every turn. My older son, Jeff, a student at Northern Michigan University and involved in Vietnam War protests, insisted in sleeping marchers on the living room floor. Exasperated and hopelessly ineffectual, I would chase them around the dining room table, flailing a hanger long before Joan Crawford made it her particular weapon. They would laugh as I consistently missed my six-foot targets.

One bright October morning, Kenny, then a sophomore at New York University, casually mentioned at breakfast that he had been wondering how I would feel if he were to tell me he was in love with a guy. Staring at him stupidly, I asked, "What do you mean—a guy?"

"Ma, you know what a guy is."

I was taken aback—nonplussed. "He overdoes this rebellion. He teases too much," I thought. What to do with a question like this? I'd ignore it, of course. But my whole body started to thump. Was he actually trying to tell me that he was Gay? I suddenly needed confirmation that he was not Gay. Not anything of the sort. He must be in some sort of post-adolescent phase. I would dial Eve, my friend the psychologist. She would soothe the thumping going on inside of me. Eve did not let me down. Sensing my need to deny Kenny's insinuating question, she was gentle. "Don't worry about it. Sometimes when a boy loses his father, he just might transfer his affection to another male. It will pass." (Later I came to realize that Eve believed as did so many in her profession in those days that homosexuality was a failure to develop along a certain "normal" course. At the time of my urgent call she was simply giving me balm—as a friend.)

Reassured that this was only a passing *fancy*, I wrapped myself in the comfort of denial (the standard reaction of a parent who has been told about a son or daughter's homosexuality).

Fortunately, I thought at the time, Kenny said no more of That Subject and as far as *I* knew was dating girls and absorbed in his studies at college. A year went by—during which time I started to date. As any divorced or widowed woman knows, the experience of middle-age dating is bewildering—and absorbing. I

4

would ask my younger brother, the family bon vivant, how to behave on dates. What should I do? What is expected? "Wing it," said my brother. And so I did, winging it all the way. What I did not know—and would not have wanted to know—was that while I was exploring modern middle-years dating mores, Kenny was exploring Gay bars and Gay life in Greenwich Village.

One night at a party I met Gene Back. I was in love again. Gene was an attorney who had been a widower for five years. We happened quickly. In the space of four months we were married. I would have liked to be "pinned" or whatever represented "going steady" in those years, but Gene was intent on legalizing us fast. (Were the dishes and laundry piled high awaiting some good woman for all those years that he was alone? Did he need a bit of help with his sixteen-year-old daughter?) But seriously and actually, Gene felt that he had gone it alone long enough and was impatient for us to start our new life together. It was a happy decision. We both felt lucky, a feeling neither of us had had in a long time.

Another year went by. There were no more hints or startling signals from Kenny, who had by now transferred to a small experimental college in Maryland, which was, in fact, an annex of Antioch College. Kenny had wanted to go out of town to school early on, but his father's illness had kept him in New York City. He hankered for independence, wanted out from the noise, pollution and the anger in the streets—as well as the hugeness and anonymity of New York University.

Gene and I had moved from Forest Hills to New York City and were involved with adjusting to our new marriage and apartment. I was preoccupied but pleased that Jeff, Kenny and Gene genuinely liked each other. When I visited Kenny in college, I was delighted to see girls—charming girls—in the picture. The summer we were married, in fact, Kenny, traveling in Greece, met an English girl who fell so madly in love with him that she left her home in London to join him in Maryland. Amanda was certainly captivated by Kenny, and Kenny seemed to return her affection. If I consciously thought of Kenny's question—"How would you feel if I were in love with a guy?"—I would have been *sure* he was teasing me. Who could be more normal, more whole-some, more heterosexual than Kenny?

Then in September, Kenny phoned from Maryland to say he was bringing a friend, Clem, home for the weekend. His voice was bland—unusually so. Often on such weekends Kenny would stay with friends, and Gene and I would meet or invite him for brunch or dinner. This time, however, his plans to visit with a childhood friend, Josh Brand—a would-be writer living in a fourth-floor Greenwich Village walk-up—went awry. Josh (who later became the originator of television's *St. Elsewhere* series) was painting his apartment that week-end, so the boys stayed in the den of our new apart-ment. It was during that particular visit that I finally consciously grasped the truth.

The early seventies were Flower Power time—the height of Hippiedom. Clem and Kenny arrived with cascading hair, shaggy beards and shredded jeans. I grimaced my distaste for *That Look*. Yet despite Clem's carefully ragged appearance, he reminded me of a painting of a Spanish cavalier: the elegance, the fine aquiline features, the dancer's grace. Yes, there was a certain grace. Little did I know as I critically took in their clothes and coiffures that this zeitgeist was trivia compared to what was soon to follow.

It struck me when the four of us—Gene, Kenny, Clem and I—were about to leave the apartment for dinner. I heard Kenny say to Clem, "Get your coat, dear." *Dear* to a man?

This endearment, plus a note of confidentiality they seemed to share, brought me up short. I had never heard men address each other in this cozy, intimate way. I was alarmed by the playful private knowledge of each other they seemed to share. In my world such affection passed between men and women.

Suddenly, I realized that Kenny and Clem were lovers!

Lovers? Oh, no.

I was unprepared to deal with this revelation. It was easier to push my new knowledge to one side—for now.

We went to a Spanish restaurant in Greenwich Village where I anesthetized myself with its ambiance: paella and long gulps of Sangria. I focused on the roving guitarists who burst into the neighborhood Spanish restaurants with impassioned renditions of "Juanita" and "Cielito Lindo" for something like three minutes every hour. The guitarists then would pass their upturned sombrero around for donations from the diners for six minutes. I laughed at a fellow who placed a bogus giant one-hundred-dollar bill in the hat.

I would not think about Kenny and Clem. I would digest the meal and the evening first. There would be plenty of time later. Eventually the evening came to an end. I said nothing about what I had perceived between the boys to Gene. But I did toss the night away so restlessly that Gene complained that he felt as though he were sleeping on a trampoline. It was a long, long night for me.

The next morning after breakfast and forced small talk on my part, I said good-bye to Gene, who left for the office, and to the two boys, who were leaving for Maryland. I told them to drive carefully. (Kenny, as usual, replied that he really did not think I should tell him what to do—that he was too old for that.) It was my day off from my job at a family planning agency. I was at last alone with it. My shame. I had a homosexual son. It was the ultimate dishonor. Kenny had decided to become a homosexual. The word "Gay" had not yet been coined for the likes of me. Instead "fag," "fairy," "pansy," "queer" rang in my ears. Derisive words. And now they applied to my son. Or did they? Perhaps I was exaggerating the boys' evident affection for each other. Overreacting.

I would check this out right now. Nervously I dialed Kenny about four and a half hours after he left for school. Kenny, not surprised, seemed in fact to be expecting my call. I fired fast.

"Kenny, tell me the truth. What's going on between you and Clem." (I could hear the accusatory tone in my voice.)

Kenny sighed.

"Okay, Mom, you've finally got it. I've been giving you signals for years, but you wouldn't see what you didn't want to see. Clem and I are lovers, and I'm Gay. I've always been Gay—and I've known since I was about ten. It's the way I am. I can't help it. It's a built-in condition like the color of my eyes."

I protested.

"But how about those girls. What about Bev? You dated her for years. Don't tell me that was nothing." How could this happen to *me*? I hoped to prove to Kenny he was mistaken.

"That was something else," Kenny said. "I was feeling my sexual way through trial and error. It's difficult to reject what you haven't tried. But now I know that I'm both physically and emotionally right with a man. I prefer men."

I felt as though I had been hit in the stomach. How could Kenny do this to me? After all the advantages we had given him—camp, out-of-town college, an MG— material advantages we had not had at his age.

My voice was choked, tight.

8

"Kenny, you cannot treat me this way. You'll see a psychiatrist or you can forget you have a mother."

SILENCE.

Kenny had hung up.

Wandering in a daze around the apartment, I felt completely disoriented. How could such a thing be happening to me? I felt alternately angry, ashamed—and guilty. Guilty. Guilty. Guilty. What had I done wrong—or was it Fred? Should I have waited until after Fred died before I told the boys about his leukemia? Should I have told them when the doctor told me? (Confronting me after Fred died, Kenny and Jeff both accused me of not telling them soon enough that their father was terminally ill. The thinking has changed, but at the time Fred was ill, it was common practice for doctors to keep a diagnosis of malignancy from their patients; in fact, many patients did not want to hear that they had cancer. I had told the boys that apparently Fred had preferred not to know: he could have pursued the truth about his condition by having his medication analyzed at a pharmacy. Some patients know that they are terminally ill but, as I pointed out to Jeff and Kenny, prefer not to talk about it. They would rather live out their remaining days close to loved ones in a nonverbal intimacy. It is a personal choice—how one decides to say good-bye.

But back to Kenny's disclosure. I denied it, I felt guilty, angry, self-righteous, indignant, wounded. I was a goulash of mixed negative feelings. During this time, I told no one—not even Gene. *Certainly not Gene*. For all his affability, Gene, as counsel for the Department of Defense, handled cases involving homosexual job applicants. If a man was a closet homosexual, the Government thought he might be amenable to coercion or blackmail. Thus, his right to security clearance could be questioned. Indeed, Gene had been criticized in the Mattachine newsletter. (The Mattachine Society, founded in 1952, was one of the earliest Gay rights groups.) I did not dare think about Gene's reaction to Kenny. *What would he say if he knew? What would he think of Kenny? What would he think of me?* I wondered what *Kenny* really thought of me. Didn't homosexuals dislike women? Did Kenny dislike me?

During the following months—still keeping Kenny's disclosure from Gene—I cast about for early traumas to explain Kenny's homosexuality. Tears filled my eyes as I bobbed up and down in the dreary waters of self-pity. I tried to roll back the years—to his childhood. Back to incidents that might account for this . . . anomaly. Did I want a girl for a second child? Did I cut his hair too late? Did I dress him in feminine clothes?

Virtuously I remembered the years of vigorous parenting when I was den mother to a bunch of eight-year-old Cub Scouts, who were always rolled into balls of scuffling arms and legs. I remembered clearly the food fights with potato chips flying through the air and the aspirin I took after each meeting. While my friends tore through Alexander's on afternoon shopping sprees, I endured those exhausting Cub Scout sessions so Kenny would be able to socialize comfortably with other little boys. How could I have known just how socially comfortable he would become with other little boys?

I recalled a birthday party when Kenny was small that might have made him anti-girl. Most of the other children—standard bearers for the local orthodontist—had their teeth wired in steel braces. During spin-the-bottle, Kenny's braces became locked in the braces of Sara, a toothy, skinny little girl. While Kenny and Sara struggled frantically to pry themselves loose from one another, the other kids taunted them with screams of laughter and snide remarks. Kenny, who would never again speak to Sara, grew grimmer and grimmer until we were able to separate them. Was that spin-the-bottle episode a turning point?

Then came adolescence—that stressful time for both parents and kids. The stiffened sheets of my sons' early teens and the basement washing machine groaning under constant use was an irritation to me. On the one hand, I resented the time wasted doing endless loads of sheets; on the other hand, as a compulsive washer, the sticky sheets were a challenge to my laundermania.

Poking my head into Kenny and Jeff's room, I would snap, "For God's sake, boys—keep your hands on top of the covers." They would reply in cool amusement, "When we're finished, Mom." I was helpless against their insistent sexuality. Both boys were— so I thought—ogling pictures of Marilyn Monroe and Raquel Welch. By now, Kenny was an excellent swimmer, winner of tennis tournaments and waterfront counselor at Camp Tamarack in the Berkshires.

Kenny, like Jeff, certainly *seemed* manly, and in no way would I or anyone else have suspected homosexuality. I would hear Kenny laughing with his friends, telling his share of dirty jokes. I could not have known at that time that this was the only way he could feel "normal." In high school, Kenny—tall, muscular, attractive (and attentive) to girls—developed a relationship with a girl named Bev. Bev and Kenny were known as boyfriend and girlfriend.

Was Kenny's "choice"—as most of us called homosexuality in those days if we referred to it at all—a reaction against me? Was it to show his displeasure at my remarriage? Did he consider my second marriage a desertion and disloyalty to his father? Was all this *revenge* on his part? How could a boy of twenty-one know anything about homosexuality? Wasn't it just another protest against authority or, in the phrase of the day, the Establishment? Kenny, I knew, would "come round" sooner or later and admit that this was a case of mistaken identity—*his*. Wouldn't he? Had I done something to drive him Gay—if Gay he really (impossibly) was? Did he catch homosexuality at summer camp? Had some sinister Gay counselor lured him into—a Gay trap?

Though I would rather have blamed Fred than myself, I nevertheless ruled him out. Even *I* had heard the phrase "distant father, controlling mother" as a cause of homosexuality, but in spite of Fred's frequent business travels, at home he was a concerned and affectionate father. Admittedly a little more neurotic and erratic that most men I knew, Fred was an Austrian who had fled from his own country during the Hitler period. He had seen the atrocities. Escaping from the perils of the Hitler regime to the perils of the U.S. Army in his mid-twenties, Fred, who spoke German fluently, was assigned to military intelligence where he was expected to interrogate German prisoners "hot off the field." The prisoners, however, were quite well treated in our camps and refused to talk to a Jew. For whatever reason, army officials tolerated this arrogance and Fred was transferred to another unit. Sustaining a back injury in the new unit, which kept him in traction for four months, Fred had also been exposed to enormous amounts of X-ray radiation. Years later when he was diagnosed as having leukemia, I read in *The New York Times* that large numbers of World War II veterans who were exposed to massive doses of X-ray radiation in the spinal area developed leukemia later on.

When the army finally discharged Fred (we met and married two years after his discharge) he opened a Ping-Pong parlor in the Times Square area. He had traveled with his Austrian Ping-Pong team in his own country and throughout Europe racking up medals. He was a wizard with his paddle. Fred could even play with a spoon or a brush, which he demonstrated when he played exhibitions at the old Roxy Theatre. When we married, he went into what he considered real work, developing an import business in Japanese ceramics. Although he traveled regularly to Japan on buying trips, Fred enjoyed recreational time with the boys. He spent long hours teaching them tennis and other sports. Fred's credo was that a true sportsman always plays to win, and he delighted in winning— even if it was only Monopoly with the boys.

Fred also brought from Vienna old-world notions of each person's role in the family.

He believed in *Respect*. Even as he lay pale and weakened by his illness in his hospital bed, Fred *demanded* Respect. When Kenny and Jeff visited him in the hospital sporting the new look of long hair, beards and ragged jeans instead of the conventional tie, sports jacket and white shirt which Fred and I both considered appropriate, Fred drew strength enough to say, "Don't come to see me again with that shrubbery on your face. Shave off the beards! When you walk into a hospital, *you must show Respect*." Kenny and Jeff, forbidden further visits until they "showed Respect," cut their hair, shaved their beards and wore neatly pressed chinos—for the time being.

How would Fred have reacted to Kenny's disclosure? With desperation, I think. He was highly emotional and would probably have been frantic. Years later, Kenny remarked that he felt his father would have "come round" on the Gay issue. Perhaps. Who knows? Maybe. He dearly loved the boys. Admittedly, Fred did adapt pretty well to a whole new life when he started over in the United States, but he would have had to work *extraordinarily* hard at revising his ideas on what was "manly."

And how about me—was I a "controlling mother"? I was a dreamy girl—not unusual in the forties and fifties—with a leaning toward the dramatic. When

I was young, the man of my dreams—yes, we actually used that expression!—would speak with a foreign accent and kiss my hand. Shades of the French actor Charles Boyer and my Latvian father. Also, I liked older men who had suffered. (That has changed.)

I had a minor ambition to act, and, indeed, I dropped out of Temple University in Philadelphia to try for a career in radio. I worked in summer stock and actually won some small parts on radio soap opera, including one line in the popular *Portia Faces Life* ("This way, please"), but my *major* ambition was to marry my fantasy man and be a wife and mother. Luckily, I thought at the time, I fell into an ideal setting where my husband was the decision maker and income producer in our household. In those days I was so conventional that I suffered not a crooked seam, never went hatless to temple, wore white cotton gloves in summer and named my kids the names of the day ("Jeff" and "Kenneth"). When I called them, the entire playground ran over to me. When Jeff and Kenny were in their teens, Klein's, a well-known discount store on Fourteenth Street in Manhattan, hired me to write advertising copy. Fred asked me not to tell anyone: "It will look like I can't support you." His concern over his husbandly status (later called "male chauvinism") was commonplace in my suburban world. In truth, I had no desire to tell anyone: my copywriting achievements ("bargains galore" was the phrase I relied too heavily upon) were few. I bring out these points to illustrate that there was no "dominant mother" but rather a dominant father. So much for Freudian theory. But now back to Kenny.

I had heard no word during these months. I realized how much Kenny had damaged my ego. I felt hurt that not only was he different from what he *appeared* to be, he was different from what I *wanted* him to be. And what about children—how would he have any? Weren't children essential? What about my friends? What would I tell them? How would I boast of his accomplishments? How would Kenny fit into my scheme of life? Would Kenny walk alone through life? What about the police? Did they entrap homosexuals, raid bars, bust heads? Would Kenny be a pariah?

How would he socialize? And with whom? (I was, of course, completely unaware of the existence of Gay bars and organizations and of the networks whereby Gay people find each other.)

What would the world do to my son?

For all my pretensions to sophistication and liberalism, my thoughts on homosexuality were limited to visions of lisping and mincing dandies. A play Gene and I attended depicting the depravity and wantonness of Gays did nothing to cheer me up. Homosexual men, I assumed, were always ridiculous caricatures of women: sissified, effeminate, weak, comic, *tragic*. As far as I knew, these depraved creatures hung out in dark, steamy bars, emerging only to swish around as hairdressers or interior decorators. In no way did Kenny fit this stereotype.

Months passed without word, but I felt that Kenny would eventually call. You don't give up a loving, understanding mother on a whim—do you?

One day the phone rang. It was Kenny, his voice uncertain, tentative:

"Hi, Mom, are you still my mother?"

Something caught at my innards. I crumbled inside. Had I actually turned away my son because he was honest and trusting enough to tell me who he was? And did it matter? Kenny was still the same boy I had raised. My son. Jeff's brother. So he had another dimension hitherto unknown to me. I would *make* it known to me. Explore on my own.

"Mom, are you there?" Kenny's voice was insistent.

"Sure, sure, Kenny. Of course. I'm still your mother. What could ever change that?"

"Mom, you'll work it out. You'll see, you just need time."

After Kenny and I hung up, I weighed my options. I made some decisions. We had always been close, and I would not lose my child because he was Gay. I would become familiar with this side of his nature. I would confront the unknown and unfamiliar—this way of life. Difficult as it would be to make the effort, I would try. At that time *(as is true today)*, parents did not have to be in psychoanalysis or consciously aware of Freudian theory to feel responsible for their children's "flaws": alcoholism, criminality, poor athletic ability, stuttering—*perversion*. So, like so many parents, I wondered what I had done. Where did I go wrong? Had I invested too heavily in Kenny's life? Had I been too controlling? Had my zealous efforts at den mothering been simply an excuse to hover over him? Was I unwittingly seductive? Too casual about religion?

Although I certainly did not have enough insight to answer these questions, I was now willing to investigate the Gay world. I was now intent on searching out the meaning of Gay: *what* was Gay, *who* was Gay, *why* was Gay and *where* was Gay? At that time, the neighborhood bookstores in Forest Hills carried only one book on homosexuality—*The Well of Loneliness* by Radclyffe Hall, a sensational novel of Lesbian love set in Paris and England in the twenties (banned on two continents!), which I had read (along with *Lady Chatterley's Lover*) in my teens. Now at the library thirty years later, I found myself rereading the haunting passages that had played such a large part in the development of my homophobic attitude: homosexuality was a mysterious blight contracted by poor unfortunates. Here in front of me were some of those discomforting passages that confirmed my biases—about female homosexuality, anyway.

> "But then Stephen [the heroine!] is very unusual, almost—well, almost a wee bit *unnatural*—such a pity, poor child, it's a terrible drawback: young men do hate that sort of thing, don't they?"
>
> "... At garden parties [Stephen] was always a failure... ill at ease and ungracious... there was something about her that antagonized slightly..."
>
> "A young woman of her age to ride like a man, I call it preposterous."
>
> "What am I, in God's name [thought Stephen] —*some kind of abomination.*"

I was obviously not doing well on my own as a student of homosexuality. One day, thank God, the only friend in whom I had confided about Kenny suggested that I see a friend of hers, Robert Laidlaw, M.D., a psychiatrist who was founder of the American Association of Marriage and Family Counselors, a member of the original Kinsey research team and (I was told) one of the few physicians who was expert in handling cases of homosexuality and sexual and gender problems. By now desperately insecure, ashamed and depressed, I called Dr. Laidlaw's office for an appointment—and I wanted one, I remember saying, *as soon as possible.* Ironically it was I—guilty, angry, shocked, threatened and confused—who saw the psychiatrist for what today is called short-term crisis therapy. Dr. Laidlaw, who was confined to a wheelchair at the time, resembled Franklin Delano Roosevelt—the hero of my youth. I liked and trusted him immediately. It was serendipity, for he was of enormous help to me.

As we talked, he compared my feelings of denial and isolation, anger, guilt—and depression (and what

he hoped would become ultimate acceptance of *loss*)—
to the staging theory expounded by Elizabeth Kubler-
Ross to explain the process of mourning.* Dr. Laidlaw
defined terms, answered questions as they popped into
my mind and suggested Gay affirmative reading. When
I first told him that it might have been better if Kenny
had never told me about himself, Dr. Laidlaw explained
that I would one day respect Kenny's courage for
taking responsibility for his life despite the societal
pressures to conform. In some ways, said Dr. Laidlaw,
it would have been easier for him to be defined by my
expectations—in fact, he went on, many homosexuals
do marry and have children, but in yielding to convention, they often pay a devastating price. He almost
convinced me that I would eventually appreciate Kenny's
trust. But at that time, I was certainly dubious. During
my therapy, fears and questions continued to spill out
one after the other.

Was Kenny abnormal?

Homosexuality is neither abnormal, uncommon nor
harmful, Dr. Laidlaw told me, and, in fact, the American Psychiatric Association was about to remove the
"sick" label from their lexicon. A few months later, in
May 1973, the *Diagnostic and Statistical Manual of Mental
Disorders*, published by the American Psychiatric Association and known as the bible of mental health
professionals, stated:

> Homosexuality per se is one form of sexual behav-
> ior and with other forms of sexual behavior which
> are *not by themselves* psychiatric disorders . . .

*On Death and Dying, (Macmillan, 1969).

Two years later, the American Psychological Association passed the following resolution:

Homosexuality per se implies no impairment in judgment, stability, reliability or general social or vocational capabilities.

(At *that* time—and today—reports on government, clerical and societal views were less reassuring.)

What caused Kenny's homosexuality? Is there a cure? Can he change? Is it a phase?

Dr. Laidlaw told me that there is no known reason why one child in a family develops a homosexual orientation and another one a heterosexual orientation, but since homosexuality is neither a disease nor an illness (or even neurosis) *it has and needs no cure.* Furthermore, he told me, most psychiatrists have failed in their attempts to convert their homosexual patients to heterosexuality. Being Gay is not just a stage that youngsters go through, and no scientific evidence backs up the claims of those who say there is a cure, nor has objective research been conducted to back up such claims. Dr. Laidlaw thought I would be interested in reading two comments on the *rights* of homosexuals to *remain* homosexual. The first, by Franklin Kameny, Ph.D., a fighter for Gay and Lesbian rights, on the *ethics* of trying to change a person's sexual orientation follows:

If the disadvantages, disabilities, and penalties which the homosexual faces are a result of society's prejudices and, of course, they are, in their entirety— then suggesting that the homosexual improve his lot by submission to those prejudices, at the cost of his personal integrity, is fundamentally immoral. One does not propose to solve the problems of anti-Semitism by conversion of Jews to Christianity much as this might improve the life of many individual Jews. The homosexual has a right to remain a homosexual, and in fact a moral obligation to do so, in order to resist immoral prejudice and discrimination.

And from George Weinberg, Ph.D., author of *Society and the Healthy Homosexual*:

...from what I have seen, the harm to the homosexual man or woman done by the person's trying to convert is multifold. Homosexuals should be warned. First of all, the venture is almost certain to fail, and you will lose time and money. But this is the least of it. In trying to convert, you will deepen your belief that you are one of nature's misfortunes. You will intensify your clinging to conventionality, enlarge your fear and guilt and regret. You will be voting in your own mind for the premise that people should all act and feel the same way. Your attempt to convert is an assault on your right to do what you want so long as it harms no one, your right to give and receive love or sensual pleasure without love, in the manner you wish to.

About this time, I ran across a statement by John Money, Ph.D. (who had suggested that one's sexuality is set, like handedness, early on). Dr. Money, Professor of Medical Psychology, Department of Psychiatry and Behavioral Sciences, Johns Hopkins University School of Medicine, author/editor of fourteen books and over 200 papers in the field of sex research, wrote:

"Until the determinants of the complete sequence of human psychosexual differentiation have been discovered, any claim to be able to intervene and influence the outcome will be based not on theoretical logic, but on trial-and-error probability. This means that any claim to be able to change homosexuality into heterosexuality will be only as valid as the validity of its counterpart, namely, the claim to be able to change heterosexuality into homosexuality."

So much for any thought of luring Kenny back to what I considered "normal."

Would Kenny have any friends now? Would he go through life with no one in our social strata to keep him company?

Kenny would be isolated and alone, I told Dr. Laidlaw. Friendless. By rejecting all that was normal (as we refer to the nuclear family), Kenny would leave us all behind. Mother. Brother. Grandparents. None of us could follow and share his life in his netherworld. I would not understand the language—verbal or nonverbal. It would be a secret society, and I would be locked out. Dr. Laidlaw told me that at the last Kinsey research team count, the figures turned up 20 million Gay people who come from every culture, religion, ethnic group and every occupation. The Kinsey study estimated that 10 percent of the population is homosexual and that Gay people and their families represent one-third of the people in this country. One out of every four families has a Gay member. "Hmmm," I thought, relieved. "Then Kenny will have friends if there are so many like him." *How* they would find each other I still could not imagine.

What if I have to listen to jokes and put-downs about "faggots" and "queers" at parties?

The good doctor told me I did not have to listen or to laugh at "homophobic name-calling." If I did not think remarks were funny, I could say so. If I was annoyed, I could walk away, change the subject, take issue with the name-caller, or reveal myself as the mother of a Gay son. I had choices. I would never have guessed that years later I would find myself drawn into hot arguments at parties when the subject came up. I would notice people looking at me sideways, but would no longer care.

What about promiscuity? What about stability?

Although we hear a lot about one-night stands and sordid Gay bars, many Gay men are really looking for stable relationships, and many achieve them, said Dr. Laidlaw. He conjectured that as the heterosexual world becomes more accepting of homosexuality, many more Gays will be in exclusive relationships. Besides, as he pointed out, look at the divorce statistics (and in the early seventies the statistics showed a lower divorce rate than now) which reveal that *hetero*sexuality is not an assurance of enduring relationships.

If Kenny is in a relationship with a man, does one act the male (active) and the other female (passive)?

Most male *and* female homosexual couples are not bound by such role-playing, Dr. Laidlaw told me. (Several months later, when I began to meet Kenny's Gay friends, I could see that indeed there was little aping of traditional roles.) So many people ask me now, "Who plays the man?" "Who plays the woman?" The answer: neither. How Kenny and Sam, Kenny's lover, manage their domestic life is a matter of individual talent and taste. Usually—certainly in the case of Kenny and Sam—their home counts very much. They both enjoy music, theater, friends—all the pleasures that add up to a rich life. Because many openly Gay men bring in two incomes and are not involved in child care, they have more to spend on material things. Kenny and Sam do aspire to as comfortable a life-style as they can afford. Their friends are both Gay *and* straight. Kenny and Sam are involved not only with their own families but with each other's. (Sam, for instance, was a pallbearer at my father's recent funeral.)

But isn't homosexuality unnatural?

I was astonished to learn that homosexuality has existed in every society since time began, and in many societies it has been more acceptable than in our own. "There is probably no culture from which homosexuality has not been reported," writes Drs. Clellan Ford and Frank Beach in *Patterns of Sexual Behavior* (Harper and Row). No matter how it has been morally frowned upon or legally prohibited, it persists—and the incidence of homosexuality is greater in countries that forbid it than those which accept it! Dr. Laidlaw added that homosexuality is not "chosen," not "selected" —but rather *"discovered."*

What about a profession for Kenny? What about discrimination?

In no way did I expect an easy answer on that. Dr. Laidlaw told me that I would be surprised to know that homosexuals contribute to every profession and occupation at every economic and social level and if I did not know this, most likely the reason was because as yet most homosexuals were still in the closet. I was worried that Kenny, now majoring in psychology, would encounter difficulties in graduate school and later on in private practice. Dr. Laidlaw explained that not only were the behavioral sciences more accepting of homosexuals than many other fields, but some of the best scientific research on sexuality was being done by Gay psychologists and scientists. Actually, he believed—correctly as it turns out—that Gay men and women were becoming less limited in the kinds of careers they could pursue. (Much of this was in response to my type-casting of Gay hairdressers and interior decorators.)

Times were changing. New books were being published by Gay and non-Gay presses, and the range of reading was greatly expanded from a year or so earlier when I prowled the Queens public library only to find *The Well of Loneliness* and a few mentions of homosexuality in *Abnormal Psychology*. I began to pour over *The Same Sex*, a group of essays on homosexuality edited by Ralph W. Weltge, in which I found a passage by Wardell B. Pomeroy, Ph.D., who had been on the staff of the Institute for Sex Research with Kinsey and Laidlaw. This particular passage reinforced the affirmative feelings that were beginning to stir in me:

> Homosexuality is no respecter of age, religion or social level. It occurs as frequently among physicians, psychiatrists, clergymen, judges and politicians as among truck drivers and ditch diggers.
>
> If my concept of homosexuality were developed from my practice, I would probably concur in thinking of it as an illness. I have seen no homosexual man or woman in that practice who was not troubled, emotionally upset, or neurotic. On the other

hand, if my concept of marriage in the United States were based on my practice, I would have to conclude that marriages are all fraught with strife and conflict and that heterosexuality is an illness. In my twenty years of research in the field of sex, I have seen many homosexuals who were happy, who were participating and conscientious members of their community and who were stable, productive, warm, relaxed and efficient.

What about danger?

Dr. Laidlaw could *not* be so reassuring about danger—and my fears. This fear was not unrealistic. I knew about the resistance to Gay rights bills in this and other cities; that there were such terrorists as "fag bashers" lurking in the shadows of Gay areas and elsewhere; that there was blackmail committed against those Gays who were closeted; that there was job discrimination; that there was the threat of fire-and-brimstone from assorted clergy; that too many among us pointed accusing fingers. I shivered.

After a few months in therapy, my anxiety had subsided enough for me to tell Jeff and Gene about Kenny. The nature of Gene's work had added to my reluctance to tell him about Kenny. However, to my relief and surprise, he merely said, "So what? He's still Kenny." Jeff, who opened my eyes to the fact of the ease with which many young people were starting to accept their siblings as Gay, said, "What else is new?" I wondered if the parent was usually the last to know.

Kenny, now openly Gay, had completed his master's in psychology and had decided to remain in Maryland. He purchased a tiny four-room house without running water in a wooded area called Hidden Acres. Shortly after he took title he had a perk test done and splash—water! The builder in him surfaced. He and other friends built a bathroom to end all bathrooms. It was enormous—with shrubbery, bunk beds and stained-glass windows. The improvements he made turned what had been not more than a cabin into a warm, cozy home.

Now that I had become increasingly more comfortable with the fact of Kenny's being Gay, Gene and I would occasionally drive to Maryland to visit. Since I was enormously relieved by Gene's casual response and subsequent supportiveness, I also told my two brothers and selected friends. They were, of course, not only surprised but shocked, mostly because Kenny (who at that time was working for the state as a psychologist) seemed so typically male. When I met his friends, I saw that some of them were a bit *femme*, but I could now see them as nonthreatening, fun-loving, healthy people with a double-edged wit (which no doubt arises from presenting one face to each other and another to the world). Most, however, were *not* discernibly Gay, and I saw them as people who want what we all want: love, intimacy, acceptance, a home, friendship, and success. Gradually, at holiday times Kenny and his Gay friends blended into our family celebrations. As my awareness of the Gay world expanded, my anger became redirected: I was no longer angry at Kenny, but at the heterosexual society that sneers at and rejects homosexuality.

I experienced a series of dawnings.

I began to challenge old stereotypes.

I began to challenge bigoted views on life.

I began to think for myself.

As I moved forward over the years (often with two steps forward and three steps backward), I could hardly believe the change in me. I ceased to do a double take when Kenny and Sam kissed in greeting at the end of the day. I hid a smile when Kenny placed a flower from the bud vase on the table next to the tip for a particularly handsome Gay waiter—and when my parents visited Kenny and Sam with Gene and me, I helped Kenny reverse their shower curtain from the naked male side to the naked female side.

I remember the time I read a Gay newspaper, *The New York Native*, on the bus, and the woman next to me craned her neck in shock. Just recently, when a good friend and neighbor said that "those faggots in *La Cage aux Folles* were so goddamned gorgeous that they gave me a hard-on and I was embarrassed about it," I did not even flinch.

Most satisfying of all have been my talks with Kenny (who was pleased that *I* went for therapy). The talks began when I was still seeing Dr. Laidlaw. At last, we really talked. We talked about his terrible internal emotional struggle to accept his own homosexual fantasies. I asked questions. Kenny answered them. I expressed my feelings. Kenny listened. We communicated as adults.

Kenny told me that being Gay was as much a part of him as his right-handedness, his blue eyes and his aesthetic sense. It was, he said, an immutable fact of his life—and *a fact with which he was happy*. (I think of the Gay author Christopher Isherwood's words: "I have been perfectly happy the way I am. If my mother was responsible for it, I am grateful!") Kenny said he learned the traditional values of heterosexual life-styles in all the same ways as Jeff and his friends by modeling after his parents, watching television and reading, *yet he knew at age ten* that he was a budding homosexual. When the other boys were just reading comic books, Kenny was secretly ogling the physiques of the body builders on the backs of the comic. He knew enough to say nothing to anyone, thinking that he would magically outgrow his fantasies about men. He knew his feelings would have created a crisis in our traditional family, and he did not dare risk "coming out" until his first serious homosexual relationship in college. I feel ashamed when I think back on my reaction to Kenny's coming out at nineteen—and yet how could I possibly have understood then?

I had not been aware of the Stonewall riots in New York City, Gay Liberation or Gay student organizations on campuses. I could find very little on the subject of homosexuality in the bookstores and libraries. I was surprised when Kenny told me that Gays who grew up alien and isolated discovered each other in the same ways that Gene and I did—through prolonged glances; animated, curious conversation; slow, cautious self-revelation. Kenny told me that in those college days, new friends—Gay friends—were becoming family to him—family that he could be truly honest with and who would not reject him. But it was not until his second year in college that he met a young man with whom he became infatuated. He realized then that he was separating from me emotionally, and only the truth between us could help reestablish our family ties.

So when Kenny said, "What would you say if I were in love with a guy?" he wanted to share with me and at the same time rid himself of the guilt and shame he had privately endured throughout the past decade. He wanted to get close to me and let me in on his life. As he describes it, I was "taken aback" (to say the least!), reserved in my reaction, confused and at a loss as to what to do with the information. Clearly, I gave him the message that I did not accept his honesty and that this was a subject which we must avoid.

Kenny was disappointed in my inability to cope with the truth. He felt that this information was *the* important fact for me to know about his life and that I was unable to handle it. In the following years, Kenny told me he had only shared with me whatever was relatively superficial. He had kept quiet about his sexual/romantic development. My refusal to ask questions, to become informed, to take the lead in preserving our relationship led him to question his identity, and so, his dating of girls as well as boys continued far too long. What *I* remember are the pretty girls.

Voluptuous feminine types. There was one whom he dated for a number of years. One day her mother called me to tell me that they had broken up and that her daughter was locked in her room "crying her eyes out." "Why?" I wanted to know. I got double-talk. Finally, a muffled, "Ask your son. I can't bring myself to tell you the reason." She hung up. I had known her casually, but when next I saw her she averted her eyes and ignored me.

Kenny was noncommittal about the breakup. "We used each other up. There was nowhere to go. It's over." (I forgot about it.)

Kenny, feeling betrayed by my response, knew he was not crazy and was not going to see a psychiatrist. I, who had raised him to be as truthful as possible, saw his confession as a weapon with which he had deliberately hurt me rather than as a fact of his life. I wondered how I could ever again be proud of his accomplishments.* I vividly recall my acute discomfort when he quite rightly told me: "You couldn't get far enough away from yourself to attempt to understand who I was or what I had gone through."

Kenny had seen my reaction as a demand for "emotional reimbursement." He was to paint himself

---

*I am proud now. At thirty-three, Kenny is a licensed psychologist, director of a successful urban private practice, and Chairman for the Committee on Gay Concerns of his state psychological association. He is the founder and president of a large, mostly Gay, business and professional association, has built his own home with the help and loving support of his lover of over six years, and is openly identified in his community as Gay. He has strong emotional bonds with his family, friends, professional associates and "in-laws." By most standards (mine included), his life-style would be considered "successful" (if not superior).

into the picture I had envisioned for him: a straight, successful young man who would live an exciting life with riches, international travel and a charming young woman on his arm. He believes that parents who see their children as extensions of themselves wish to bask vicariously in their glory. These parents—I was one of them—want to get "paid back" for the years devoted to the children. Kenny told me that when parents have this preconceived idea of how their child is going to reimburse them emotionally, *homosexuality surely does not fit into the picture*. I began to see Kenny as an individual—not as a person whose job on earth was to live up to *my* expectations. He must live his own life in the best way he could find. As I started to acknowledge the real Kenny and we both abandoned our old roles, we grew much closer.

In the years that followed, I saw that the Gay population was banding together to gather strength. I saw the upsurge. I decided that it was time for a bit of an upsurge on my part. Although I had been working in public relations and counseling in a family planning center, I thought more and more about the problems of families of Gay people. Finally, I decided to stop thinking and move on it.

First I would need to complete my long-forsaken undergraduate degree; then, I would need a master's degree in social work.* I saw that the concerns of families of Gay people had not yet been properly dealt with by social work professionals.

Miraculously, Fordham University accepted me—even at what I considered my advanced age—and there I remained until I had completed their requirements for a master's, graduating twice in four years and becoming a bore and a chore to my family and friends with this hitherto undemonstrated interest in

*I had a counseling certificate from the New School of Human Relations.

academia. It was gratifying to see and be with many other midlife career-switch-syndrome students. Not that I was faced with a sea of gray in class, but it was reassuring to sit next to a once-famous, now seriously bespectacled and pigtailed stripper in my statistics class.

I was now willing to stand up and be counted—next to my Gay son.

When I started at Fordham, Kenny was in California working on his doctorate. That was when I met Sam. It was Christmas 1980. On this shining day, standing on Kenny and Sam's apartment balcony facing Balboa Park in San Diego, we looked out on the Spanish-style exhibition halls—reminders of the time the park was the site of the Panama-California International Exposition in 1915–16. The Del Prado glittered with Christmas decorations; bare-chested runners in shorts streaked by; children and adults sent up bright-colored kites into the sky. It was an especially Southern California scene, a *sharp* contrast to the cold, snowy, bleak Christmas landscape of Philadelphia where I grew up and the New York of my adult years.

Inside we celebrated the season with a mix as totally unlike the magazine covers of the traditional family—Pa carving, Ma serving—as one could imagine. Instead, this holiday cast included the hosts—my son Kenny and his lover Sam, a medical resident—my husband Gene, my son Jeff and his then-wife Elizabeth, their three-year-old daughter Emmanuelle (and other small children), Sam's recently separated parents (each accompanied by dates), a Gay attorney from London, several medical students (both Gay and straight), a Naval commander, several nonmedical people, a few elderly people who lived in the same apartment house. Conversation sparkled; the food—each person brought his or her specialty—was superb. While sipping champagne in the glow of good fellowship, I saw this scene as a microcosm of the world in all its diversity. This was as it should be. Peace on earth. Good will toward men. *All* men.

How did I feel when I met Sam? Was I embarrassed? What did I think of him? Actually (status-conscious as I was in those days), I beamed my approval. Sam was a third-generation Californian and a medical doctor, no less. If Kenny had to have a male lover instead of a pretty young wife, at least he was a doctor.

Sam is a Renaissance man. Articulate and gentle, he has a lovely sense of whimsy and fun. People warm to Sam. That Christmas, after untold hours of interning at the Veterans Hospital, he came home and started to string popcorn and spruce up the plants. His hands are never idle. Does it sound as though I like Sam? I do. I feel Kenny and Sam are lucky to have found each other, and I hope that their relationship grows and endures. (As I write this—six years later, Sam, having completed his medical residency, is now a full-fledged R.D. [real doctor!]). He and Kenny have moved to Baltimore where they've built this push-button electronic "Star Wars" kind of house, supervising every detail of its construction.

Sam volunteers as medical director of the Gay Men's Health Center, is the Medical director of a nursing home and is on the staff of a major Baltimore hospital. (Sam says of the nursing home that he likes making this last stop as comfortable as possible for the octogenarian and nonagenarian occupants.) He tells the story of how his patients seem to like him very much. That is, when they can see him! Most approach him nose to nose and then greet him with, "Hello there, Father." (Sam reminds them that a doctor wears a white coat; a priest wears a black coat.) Gene and I have already reserved our room there.

During that Christmas holiday, I noticed how Sam's background was so very different from Kenny's. As told to me by Sam, his father was born in Kansas, the oldest son of conservative Baptist parents. Their home was built on conservative fundamentalist beliefs; dancing, parties and card-playing were frowned upon. When Sam's father was in his early twenties, he joined the navy and was stationed in San Diego. After the navy tour of duty, Sam's dad met his mother while they were both in college. They married and had four children. Sam told me that his father was demonstrative and loving—characteristics that his father's parents had lacked. Sam's father, who rose in his teaching career to become a school principal, loved golf and was "especially good at it." Despite time spent on the golf green, he and Sam shared an avid interest in gardening and together tended the garden.

Sam's mother, raised a Presbyterian, also raised their children in the liberal Christianity of the Presbyterian church. Her family—gold prospectors, forest rangers, farmers and freight wagon drivers—settled in San Diego. A cousin chronicled Sam's grandmother's memoirs (on his mother's side) which tell about her early days in California and had the book carefully bound. It was passed around to family members and is dearly cherished. His grandmother's house in Lakeside, a small town in the outskirts of San Diego, still stands as the town grew up around it. Sam's relationship to his grandmother was very special and I recall the frequent trips he made to the hospital to visit her before she died.

Sam, the second oldest in his family, told me that as a child he was very close to his older sister. Because the salaries of teachers were low, Sam and his brothers and sister grew up with few material luxuries. Often, they improvised their own games. Unable to afford a television in its early years, Sam and his sister sat instead in front of the dryer, watching the spinning clothes and fantasizing their own stories about what was happening to Howdy Doody and other television characters of their day. "That dryer was certainly instrumental in developing my imagination," said Sam. Perhaps those early years of finding an alternative to not having a real TV enabled Sam to develop his knack of taking reality and going it one better. He was able to take society's reality and substitute it for his own. Sam dreams of a world where people will not be affronted because of the difference in their orientation.

Unlike Kenny, who had told me that he became aware of his homosexual feelings when he was about ten, Sam was unaware consciously of his own inclinations until he was in college and in his early twenties. Attending a small church college in Iowa and active in the drama club, the school band and other extracurricular activities, Sam's friends were both men and women. "I did a pretty good job of suppression," Sam said. "I never gave my crushes on men a name." As he remembers, his feelings toward men were strong but he was unable to come to terms with the idea of being homosexual.

"When I finally did come to terms after a brief fling with a classmate, I felt relieved. I could put the pieces together and see where I was. I graduated in 1975, and before I left the country to teach English in France, I wrote my father a letter.

"Dad wrote in reply that he was not all that surprised and was glad I told him. We were able to talk about anything, and this confirmed the love we felt for each other. In his letter he wrote that what I had revealed would not diminish the love and caring between us and that I would always be his son.

"Until his letter arrived, I was anxious and filled with trepidation. Yet I felt that I had taken a positive step in life. I had jumped a hurdle. I had a sense of accomplishment. My father asked me not to tell my mother. I felt he had underestimated her capacity for understanding and her love for me, but I agreed to abide by his wishes. Unwillingly. After all, I had my own relationship with her. When my mother and I finally talked about it five years later, she admitted that she knew but chose not to think about it." (Like me, Sam's mother also had her share of guilt.) She wondered about her part in producing a Gay son. Maybe she should not have let Sam putter around with her Brownie group. Maybe she should have farmed him out when the little girls met at her house. She wondered if all the artsy-craftsy paper dolls they had busied themselves with had in some way influenced Sam to become Gay.

Sam reassured her, "No, Mom. Your Brownie group had nothing to do with my being Gay. I was Gay long before that." When I met Sam's mother, she said that, like me, she had been so puzzled because Sam did not fit the homosexual stereotype. "Our family is so respectful of other people's feelings and privacy that she waited to say anything to me," Sam said. "When my parents separated in 1976 and ultimately divorced, I waited until she had sufficiently recouped before I discussed my life with her explicitly.

"At college, there was a small campus Gay support group with student and faculty members. There was even a small space on our bulletin board for Gay news. In fact, the first Midwest Gay Pride conference was held in Iowa City—and I attended."

Gene's and my relationship with Sam was to bloom. I admire not only the courage it took for him to pass the endurance tests that medical residents are put through but the courage it took to be open about himself during that time. These days, I must admit to shamelessly milking and exploiting his medical expertise. He good-naturedly puts up with my continued request to "look" at some part of me—an eye, a rash, a foot. Whatever ails.

It was during that visit in San Diego with Kenny and Sam that I started to wonder what was going on in the millions of other American homes that had spawned Gay children. Did Gay couples still in the closet perpetuate the lie by visiting their families separately? If they were out of the closet, did their families merely *endure* the holiday visit? Was the Gay couple accepted as two people like the rest of us with lovable—and unlovable— traits?

Unlikely.

Sam happens to have been born into a family almost cinematic in its representation of early Americana as historically described.

Kenny was born into a family as dissimilar as could be.

The Gay people I have met, interviewed and whose families have been members of my workshops demonstrated the difference inherent in their family of origin over and over again.

Like seeds scattered and falling in the wind, the inclination to be Gay is a haphazard and natural phenomena.

Of this I was, and am, convinced.

The day arrived when I felt ready (give or take a few twinges) to attend a Gay Pride march. This annual parade, which is also held in other large cities, marks the anniversary of the June 28, 1969, police raid on a Gay bar in Greenwich Village—the Stonewall Inn. There had been a sharp clash, and the Gays had fought back—for the first time. It is believed by many Gay people that this incident historically marked the cornerstone for the beginnings of Gay rights activism. Only partly out of the closet myself, I was disguised in huge black sunglasses and a droopy hat hung down over my nose.

I asked a young woman standing next to me what streaming lavender balloons, banners, ribbons and confetti meant. She said that lavender symbolized the blending of gender traits. Darting quick looks at the other spectators, I wondered how many of them were, like me, parents of a Gay child. Their faces told me nothing.

I looked at the vanguard—two bronzed, bare-chested, achingly beautiful boys, gliding by on roller skates, as in a slow-motion film. Their eyes scanned the crowd. What had they expected to see? Whatever—they seemed ready to deal with it.

There was a line of police officers and a double row of barricades, but the procession was orderly: the marchers divided into groups—each organization holding banner, placards (and faces) high. I inspected those faces for the stereotypical expression, the bodies for stereotypical postures.

What had I expected?

I saw only typical-looking American kids. Like mine, like anyone's.

I would never have been able to tell who was Gay had we met apart from the parade. There *were* a few men with mincing walks—just a few. There *were* strutting women—but only a few.

When the girls and women passed, chanting, "We are everywhere. We are your mothers and your fathers, your brothers and your sisters, your sons and your daughters, your aunts and your uncles. You know us well," I drew up sharply, deeply stirred.

I remember the shock—I was not ready to laugh just yet—of a Janus-faced drag queen, swaying to a mock shivaree—one-half clad in bridal finery, blond wig in place and clutching one half of a nosegay; the other side a spiffy groom, topped off with one-half of a top hat. The two-sided parody flaunted an enormous sign—"So when are you two getting married?" The lipsticked side of his mouth had been pursed in a grimace. As the onlookers roared, I had wondered how many minority groups could turn their humor around on themselves and score so deeply.

There was a loud chortle from the crowd: a cluster of Jewish Gay men were dancing to the beat of the hora, their tiny beanielike yarmulkes mysteriously adhering to their bobbing heads as they circled each other in the throb of the dance. An elderly Jewish woman had yelled, "Gae avec mitt your 'Gay' already." Laughing, they skipped around her.

Jeanne Manford, founder of Parents of Gays and Lesbians, a group that meets to share parental concerns and do battle for Gay Rights, led their float with her usual dignity and courage. I had always been awed by the strength of this sweet-faced, gentle, fourth-grade schoolteacher who obviously had steel innards when it came to her beliefs. Jeanne, whom I later interviewed for this book, actually had the moral fiber to march up Fifth Avenue in the early seventies, carrying a placard demonstrating her love and support for her Gay son, Morty—no mean feat in those years before the American Psychiatric Association declared that homosexuality was not a mental illness. This was something that I—not a heroine in this sense—could not and would not be brave enough to do.

When I did meet Jeanne Manford, she said, "I often wondered where the words came from when I spoke at Parents of Gays meetings. I'm basically shy and tend to wait for people to approach me. I don't know where I got the courage: perhaps we are meeting certain tasks in life." She recalled her principal's remark that it was unseemly for a teacher to attract public attention to herself and how she had replied that what she did on her own time and at her own risk was her concern only. From that time on, nothing was said at school about her activities with the organization. Jeanne, her tears glistening, remembered her husband, Jules, who had recently passed away, and how they had shouldered the beginnings of Parents of Gays together. Perhaps it was the fact that Morty was beaten up for distributing leaflets for Gay Rights that steeled her determination to tell the world that he was not alone and the fact that his attacker got off with a slap on the wrist. This lady has set an example for thousands of parents of Gay people to step forward, hands on the shoulders of their Gay children. During the evening we met, we talked of the problems besetting parents of Gay children. I told Jeanne how delighted I was with Sam, Kenny's lover of some years. She sighed and said, "It would be so nice if only Morty would meet someone. His life would be enriched; he would have a partner. I would be so happy if he brought home some nice fellow."

We burst out laughing, each thinking how unlikely such a conversation would have been when our sons were little boys back in the fifties.

But now I saw the marchers holding up signs that read "Dignity," the Catholic organization for Gays; "Integrity," the Protestant Episcopal organization; "Gay Christian Scientists"; "Concerned Lutherans." It went on and on. All of these people had formed separate religious groups to worship in the faith of their choice as Gay men and women.

There were young Gays helping the elderly Gays who belonged to a group called Sage for Gay senior citizens. A soccer ball was booted along the avenue; the athletes—strong, macho-looking men—lunged at the ball with bulging muscles. At that moment most of my ideas about the "Gay appearance" went askew. How does one tell who's Gay and who's straight?

Once again, on the last Sunday of June 1983, I stood on the sidelines watching the Gay Pride march, the theme of which was AIDS. I stood at the corner of 34th and Fifth Avenue taking in the faces of the tens of thousands lining the streets: well-ordered, controlled, organized. I did not wear outsize sunglasses or a large disguising hat, not this year.

Purple confetti was strewn down the avenue as far as the eye could see. The police stopped traffic every few minutes to let the marchers pass, and when an occasional motorist honked in protest, the crowd shouted, "This is our day. Wait for us!"

A few heartbeats away, I saw the unchosen: an unsmiling contingent of young men carrying their banner which read, "Gay Men's Health Crisis." An avalanche of violet-colored streamers descended on them from the buildings above as they strode in steady pace: vulnerable faces set—reflecting a grim purpose.

A man and woman in the crowd held each other tightly, as though they were braced against an unknown danger. Of what were they afraid? How sad that they had to be afraid.

I followed the marchers to the West Side Highway at 12th Street, where their rally began. The raised platform held electronic equipment and reporters. The roll call went on and on, trumpeting the names of innumerable participating organizations. A handsome woman wearing a white tunic, holding a bottle of beer aloft, made her way to the platform. It was Virginia Apuzzo, then executive director of the National Gay Task Force, which strives to insure the human dignity and rights of Gay people. Her electric delivery sent a charge through blocks and blocks thick with people. "We will not be disenfranchised! Enough is enough! The stain of shame will not be inflicted upon us because of this epidemic!" Ms. Apuzzo spoke of the potential political power that Gay people held in their hands, should they only clench their fists. She spoke of human rights. There was a moment of silence in memory of those who had died of AIDS. Suddenly the marchers released hundreds of purple balloons. Looking up I saw an umbrella of purple floating over the skyscrapers of Manhattan; I thought of a phrase from a play by the late Lesbian playwright Jane Chambers that went something like this: "I may not march, but I do not hide."

Aware that my own closet door was open, a surprising number of my friends' children approached me at various times to tell me that they were Gay. Many of them divorced—as far as their parents could see for vague reasons—were unhappy about living a charade. Still they were afraid that if they revealed themselves, they would lose their parents' love and respect. As with the other Gay people I met, they wanted and needed to keep their place in their families but were apprehensive about the outcome of disclosure.

It became more and more apparent to me that the needs of the families of Gay people were not being sufficiently attended to: that there was a wall between most Gay children and their families that prevented honest communication and created emotional distance.

I scanned the Fordham social work school catalog. Never did I come across one course on the off-limits subject of homosexuality. (This was also true of the catalogs of other universities teaching social work.) I was astonished. After all, here was an unresolved problem facing millions of people in the United States alone who had Gay family members. Most of the families were rejecting, unreconciled or ambivalent about accepting their sons and daughters as Gay. Surely these family problems were social work concerns.

Whenever possible, I used my courses to explore my favorite topic, which led me to design a questionnaire on the subject dearest to my heart—parental reaction to Gay sons. Then, I placed the following advertisement in *The New York Times*, February 10, 1980:

PARENTS OF GAY SONS. WOULD YOU DISCUSS YOUR ATTITUDES FOR ACADEMIC STUDY? ANONYMITY ASSURED. (212) 555-1234. GLORIA/55153.

I placed similar ads in neighborhood papers and on college Gay club bulletin boards, and I distributed the questionnaires among attendees at Parents of Gays support group meetings, which were led by dedicated volunteers. Although I had originally intended to connect with parents of Gay *sons* (obviously that was my special concern), parents of Lesbians contacted me, too. My interest in family reactions to Gay daughters broadened my inquiry and my interest.

I heard from parents who had never before opened up to anyone about their Gay sons and daughters. They phoned me, met me in such varied places as Bloomingdale's, parking lots, coffee shops; those who only filled out part of the questionnaire added personal notes. Having a Gay child is a great leveler. Here's what the parents—and children—told me.

What the Parents Said

Men say to us, "There is this problem of the family. How are we to preserve it? It seems to be dissolving before our very eyes." That has been true perhaps always and everywhere. Everywhere good things seem to be going. Yet everywhere they are merely struggling to their new birth.

—Bede Jarrett, *The House of Gold*

Most of the parents who responded to my ads and took part in my later workshops were white middle-class people who had tried in all good conscience to cope with their children's pain in growing up. They were ready for almost anything—cults, drug abuse, school problems—anything except a Gay child. Their reactions ranged from covering up and concealing the fact, uncomfortable *over*acceptance, patronizing I-love-you-but attitudes to out-and-out cruel rejection. A few—too few—held out their arms without qualification.

I have included the cruelest, most shocking rejections—as well as sincere acceptance of a child's homosexual orientation. And I hope that readers will not see their own situation as a crisis but rather as a challenge. Here is an opportunity to expand their horizon, learn about and meet with a new population in our very midst. (It is said that every fourth family has a Gay family member.) Best of all, readers may come to really know and understand their Gay child.

I have changed the names, locations and identifying facts about the people discussed in the following pages to preserve their privacy. I have paraphrased and selected excerpts from what they told me. Some of their stories drew my comments or evaluations—or both. Others did not because they needed none.*

THE INTERVIEWS

DR. STONE: *"Suppose it was me who was Gay"*

Dr. Nathan Stone, a proctologist, a widower and father of two sons—twenty-year-old Edward and eighteen-year-old Norman—revealed to me one afternoon, when Gene and I were visiting friends in New Jersey, a family homophobia and severe sibling rivalry. Dr. Stone confided to me that his relationship with Ed had always been fun and games; but Norman—on another wavelength—had always felt excluded. Says Dr. Stone:

"I never meant to shut Norman out, but he couldn't seem to catch on to our jokes. Norman had been closer to his mother, who died of cancer two years ago. Four months ago Ed brought a young man home, and, with his arms wrapped around his shoulder, said, 'Dad, meet Jim. He's all mine.' Ed knew I was incapable of turning against him no matter what he did or how he revealed himself.

*Except for the couple who talked about their son who died of AIDS, the subject of AIDS was not brought up by the parents. I can only guess that many parents are in the midst of working through the integration of their Gay child into their psyches and are simply unwilling to deal with this new threat.

46

"I admit that I was not overjoyed that the two were obviously lovers. I knew what a rough path lay ahead for them, but I liked Jim. They were college roommates and had a steady part-time relationship.

"My problem is that my younger son Norman feels excluded. He's furious that I'm so easy about Ed's homosexuality. This is just one more thing that Ed, I—and now Jim—share without him. Now the humor among the three of us is sort of the Gay double entendre, which makes Norman—who is on the square and pompous side—even angrier. He ignores Ed and Jim, refusing to talk to them. He accused me of accepting everything that Ed does and even yelled at me, 'How would you feel if *I* were Gay. How funny would every-thing be then?'

"I've tried to convey to Norman that I would never reject a son just because he is Gay. I have told Norman that we are a small family and have to stick together no matter what. Norman, who was unconvinced, left home. He now lives with his aunt, my sister, an old biddy to whom he has probably told everything. She must be lighting candles to save our souls. Last week, I insisted Norman come for dinner. Ed, who was in one of his cute moods, said, 'Hey, Dad, how come you never threw us a wedding? How can Jim and I furnish our own place if we don't get presents from our family? Aunt Philomena still gets loot and it's her third time around.' I said Ed should send me an announcement, and I would think about it. Norman blew his top and then slammed out of the house. He won't talk to us—and I'm sick about it."

PENNY: "Here comes the cream puff's mother"

Penny, a manicurist working now in a barber shop on the Lower East Side in Manhattan, reminded me of a lioness growling to protect her kids from torment. As difficult as life has been for this family, they huddle together for emotional sustenance. Fortunately they are all in therapy now. Penny's life, a series of stunning blows which she faces with an outwardly tough and cynical exterior, knows that her three children are Gay. Divorced seven years, she has two girls and one boy: eighteen-year-old Rona; twenty-year-old Ollie; and a twenty-two-year-old retarded son, Von. They came out to her one right after the other. However, Penny felt that because she had been a battered wife—her husband had beaten her with anything he could lay a hand on from vacuum cleaner attachments to telephone receivers—her children were turned off from male-female relationships. Her daughters, she feels, see men as violent and threatening; her son feels that women are weak. Penny says:

"Von, my son, is 'emotionally unemployable'—so I've been told at the clinic. I've picked him up too many times at the police station for loitering. When I arrive on my own to collect him, the cops jeer at me: 'Here comes the cream puff's mother.' Von tells me that they write 'cream puff' on a pizza box and hang it over his cell. Even though Von's not supposed to be locked up with straight men, they lock them all up together anyway. He's been raped in jail. His body shows evidence of it. When I come for him with my fireman boyfriend, the cops show him respect. My boyfriend is muscular, tough, manly. Then there are no cracks. Not only do I have to deal with my kids' problems, but men seem to easily sense I'm alone and vulnerable and they go for my jugular. I know that some women get taken care of, but breaks like that don't come my way.

"My daughter Ollie lived with a sixty-year-old woman who was good to her. For seven years they had an apartment near Columbia, and this woman encouraged Ollie to go back to college. Ollie was majoring in psychiatry, getting good grades and had only one year until graduation when her friend died of acute leukemia. She died in three months with Ollie by her side. While she was dying, she whispered to Ollie that Ollie should keep the furniture and belongings, complete her education and take good care of herself. The bank account was in the woman's name. Ollie cried like I never saw her cry. They had really loved each other. Then, just like an old-time movie, in came a Rudolph Rassandale of a great uncle, twirling a handlebar mustache and thundering to Ollie that he changed the locks on their apartment and that she was to return all monies spent on her or his lawyer would sue for damages. Empty threats, but Ollie was in the closet at college and scared about exposure. The uncle, who never even called when his great niece was alive because he knew she was a Lesbian, refused to allow Ollie to collect her clothes and books. He said that if she tried to get in he would have her arrested for breaking-and-entering and for corrupting the morals of his niece. How can people be so vicious? Ollie and I were both intimidated. We felt we had no chance. When we called a legal-aid information service, all we got was double talk. Ollie's friend had not thought of legalizing anything to protect Ollie. This episode hardened a shell around Ollie. Now she has a day job and goes to night school and contributes toward my rent and expenses. She has discovered Gay Rights organizations, and I think that today if anyone tried to hound her, they would have a pretty tough battle. I'm proud of her strength.

"On the other hand, my daughter Rona breaks my heart. Two years ago she had a girlfriend her own age—and I felt like I had another daughter. We talked makeup and clothes and giggled. We cooked together and I felt perfectly at home in the situation. But then they broke up and Rona took up with a forty-year-old woman who is an insensitive block of cement—and jealous of me. She doesn't want Rona to talk on the phone or visit me. And she shows off in public. She thinks nothing of cutting Rona's meat in a restaurant, nibbling her ear or pawing her neck while we wait in line at the movies. I may not know much, but I do know what belongs behind closed doors. No wonder the guy in back of us sneered, 'Look at those dykes go.'

"I live in an Italian neighborhood in Queens. The guys who hang out—a bunch of Rockys— lean against the buildings in their black leather jackets and heavy neck chains watching. When I walk down the street with my kids, they start yelling, 'Here comes fagtown.' That hurts. I don't care that my children are Gay, and I don't understand why they're treated this way. They don't hurt anyone."

MARTY: "We lifted weights together"

Marty, an ex-Marine living in a small summer resort town on the south fork of Long Island, felt his manhood threatened by a Gay son. Locked into his prejudice, Marty, who coaches football at a high school, wanted a macho son to reinforce his image in the community. He thought that eventually his son Billy would "turn back" to the straight son he wanted. Billy, recently discharged from the army for "other-than-honorable conditions" has broken his father's heart. Humiliated and furious, Marty says,

"Billy stabbed me in the back. We went to the gym to work out together, we lifted weights, we were men. We stared at girls in bikinis on the beach. I thought he was as interested as I. Then they caught him with another guy on the base. I don't know for sure exactly *what* they were doing but it was definitely sex. Billy won't say anything except to tell me that like Popeye, 'I yam what I yam and that's what I yam.' He says that he can beat the shit out of anyone he has ever met and that he knows he is all man. That even though he prefers sex with a man, he's still masculine. We're both bitter and angry. In our town the word is out and he can't get a job. I want him out of my house. I can't look at him. I can't go to the bar to drink with my friends because they all know I've got a fairy for a son. I got into a brawl when someone made a crack. His being home reminds me that I failed as a father. I gave him two weeks to find a job in the city and leave. Maybe being on his own will straighten him out. Maybe he'll come back someday with all this fag stuff forgotten."

FLO: *"I'm frightened when Stan goes to a Gay bar"*

Flo met me at a coffee shop on the Upper West Side in Manhattan near Columbia University, where she works at a synagogue. Haunted by her memories of her childhood in Hitler's Germany, Flo reacted apprehensively to her son Stan's disclosure that he was Gay. Flo says:

"When Stan told me he was Gay, the same icy fear gripped me as when I was a small child—the fear of the Nazis. Only the Nazis here would go after him wearing American faces. The Nazis here would wear the blue of the American police and the politicians would shout for his blood! Everywhere he would be despised as we were despised as Jews then. I shook in my soul for him.

"Whenever a violent crime was committed in the United States I used to look to see if the accused was a Jew; now I look to see if the accused is a homosexual. I forbid Stan to tell his father because he has a heart condition and knowledge of a Gay son would kill him. I'm frightened when I know Stan goes to a Gay bar. I'm afraid he will be attacked by those roving gangs who prey on Gays or that he'll be hurt by the police. I see pogroms against Gays like they had in Europe. I can't help it. I'm going crazy."

ROSA: "Happy Birthday"

Rosa, a darkly pretty Hispanic mother of two boys, sixteen-year-old Don and eighteen-year-old Carl, has deep convictions and a philosophy from which she draws strength in unyielding situations. I think Don is lucky she is his mother. She told Don and Carl, "We have many birthdays in life, so that when we discover something new and meaningful in our lives it becomes a part of us and is therefore another birthday." On the park bench near the office where she works part-time as a billing clerk, Rosa told me:

"I have been separated from my husband for many years. We never got along. Don and Carl have been my responsibility both physically and financially. I had never met a Gay that I was aware of—or knew much about what it meant to be Gay—but after I broke up with my husband, I worked as a secretary to a Gay man in the import business. I noticed—how could I help it?—that the woman in his life was his mother. He would ask me to shop for holiday cards and gifts for his father and friends, but he took care of his mother's presents himself. Once his mother confided in me that she did not mind that her son was Gay. Now she would never lose him to another woman. Is this how she consoles herself? Does she mean it?

"About my kid: I saw that Don was different when he was five years old. He was emotional and cried easily. He was gentle when he played with other children and with his toys. He always preferred to play with little girls. He had those G.I. Joe dolls that were 'okay' for boys to play with in the sixties. Don had miniature furniture and tiny clothes for them, creating an ordered world that he never saw at home. His brother Carl would throw the dolls around or ignore them.

"When Don was nine, the teacher told me he had a mild reading disorder, dyslexia, but it would reverse itself when he was older. She suggested we take Don to a psychiatrist at the Columbia Presbyterian clinic. Don underwent a battery of tests at the clinic, but then I withdrew him because I thought the doctor was Gay. He was

53

swishy and I was afraid he'd come on to Don. That was the end of the therapy. In retrospect, I must have sensed that Don was Gay. After all, he was my kid and we were close. I felt that the doctor's homosexuality might be contagious, too. Now I know I acted protectively to head off what deep down I knew existed already. In high school, years later, Don became interested in the theater—especially dance. One day he brought home a friend. What a creature! Flashy, weird clothes, beads, bleached multicolored hair. This kid—a real creep—announced to me that he was Gay, and anyone who was Gay should come right out and say so. To be proud of it. He was in the drama and dance group with Don, and Don had already spoken of him. But God, what he looked like! When the kid left, I stormed into Don's room and forbade him to ever see the boy again. Don was lying in bed and turned his face away from me. He didn't answer. The next day Don broke out into a crazy flamboyance of his own: sequined jeans, earrings and silver shoes. Carl, who was attending the same school, complained bitterly to me. He said he was ashamed in front of his friends and that if Don didn't shape up he—Carl—would pin him to the wall.

"I knew the moment of truth had come. I flew at Don, who was, as usual, lying brooding on his bed. Only he got to me first, yelling louder. 'Damn it, Mom, cut the bullshit. I'm Gay. You know it and you've always known it. Why are you trying to hide the truth from yourself?' My heart sank. I felt that this scene had been played before.

"'Don, you're so young,' I said. 'Only fifteen. Give yourself a chance to grow up and find your way.' But deep down I knew that he had found his way a long time ago. He was only telling me what we both knew. He said, 'Mom, you just never wanted to believe your own feelings.' I gave in. Caved in.

"Then I took a deep breath. 'Okay,' I said. 'So you're Gay. Congratulations. Happy birthday!'

"Don said, 'Yeah, today's my birthday. Today I came out officially.'

"But I took a stand. Don was still a minor. I said, 'Don, you want to play it Gay? Play it Gay, but you are going to be Gay with dignity or I am going to kick in those jewels of yours. You don't need the crazy clothes or the big beads. You can be yourself without making yourself a target for fag-haters and cops. You are getting a part-time job, decent marks, you are going to dress with some restraint and I will be there to help. But if you cross me, if you bring shame to me, I will be the first to help put you away. While you live off me and with me, we're going to hold our heads up.'

"'Soon enough you'll be out there. And I won't be able to protect you.' Well, he listened. For now. I don't know what's in store for him. I had become a born-again Christian, but when the pastor denounced homosexuality from the pulpit, I left the church.

"I feel good that at least through Don's adolescent years he didn't have to carry the secret alone. I admit that I wish to God Don were straight, but wishing won't help. Carl and Don are far apart. I had always hoped they would be close, but now, there goes one more dream. Thank God, that for now at least, Don is Gay with dignity."

FRANK: "I won't be made to feel guilty"

Frank, a neighbor of mine who lives year-round in the upstate New York town where Gene and I spend our summers, told me that his twenty-five-year-old son, Dean, had come out to him a few weeks ago, and that Dean told his mother a few days later. Dean, a retail store manger, lived at home. His lover also worked at the store. Frank had his problems in dealing with the situation but did a lot of reading about Gay life and said that he felt that if Dean would just grow up and take responsibility for himself, life would be easier for all of them. Homosexuality was not the problem. The problem was that Dean was testing his parents in wanting the comforts of childhood by having his laundry done at home, eating meals at home, having parental nurturing and inviting his lover to live in his parents' home. Frank says:

> "Even though Dean has an impressive title, he earns very little. He wants his lover to live with us. Never. That I won't agree to. The fellow is pleasant enough, but when Dean brought him home last weekend, I froze every time I passed Dean's bedroom and thought of what was going on between the two. This house belonged to my parents, and I've lived in it all my life. Dean had anything he wanted growing up: his own phone, his own TV, even the use of our charge cards. Now I feel exploited. With their combined salaries, the boys can find their own place. My home is my castle. My wife tells me I'm throwing my son out, but I won't be made to feel guilty. I feel that Dean's sex life, strange as it is to me, is his own and has no place in my house."

BEN: *"My wife is as repelled and afraid as I am"*

Amy and Ben Tanner, a Westchester couple who both taught school, met me for dinner ten days after they had seen my ad in *The Times*. They were both implacable in their opposition to accepting their nineteen-year-old son Byron as Gay. Clinging stubbornly to the image of Byron as straight, they both admitted that they had counted on him to make up for the deficiencies of their sixteen-year-old daughter Bea, an epileptic, and seventeen-year-old Paul, who was retarded. It appeared beyond Ben to accept that other people might be comfortable about their children's Gayness. Rigid and unbending on the subject of homosexuality, it was apparent that if given the chance, he would live vicariously through Byron. Ben says:

"Why can't he stifle it? Do these kids have to indulge themselves in everything and anything the minute they get an impulse? Can't they deny themselves anything in consideration of the ideals and values we tried to teach them? I am positive Byron could have chosen to be heterosexual—that his going 'Gay,' as he so quaintly puts it, is his way of fighting me. I have told him that self-expression when it battles the roots of society does not guarantee happiness. I told him that happiness comes from loving a nice girl. To live as he was raised to live in a married, family state. There is no other acceptable norm to me. Byron has dated beautiful girls. He even told us he had sex with them. He is looking for thrills and he is getting back at us for having to pay so much attention to the two younger kids. He will not understand that they needed us much more than he did. He was the 'normal' one. Sure, they broke his toys and harassed him while they were growing up. But they were the disadvantaged ones. We had to give in to them more. We counted on Byron to carry on some sort of normal family tradition.

"My wife is as repelled and afraid as I am. We're both outraged that we invested so much in hopes for this boy and now he's a stranger. We seem to be holding on to—and supporting—each other. Our marriage is tighter. In the final analysis, it is just the two of us. We had hoped Byron would take some responsibility for his brother and sister, but now that's out of the question. Byron is angry that we didn't institutionalize Paul. He says that we sacrificed him for Paul—but I don't agree with that.

"Grandma—my wife's mother—who never liked me, happens to be 100 percent behind Byron. When Byron threatened to become a Krishna, Grandma said she would bob up and down with him on Fifth Avenue and help them chant. My wife says Grandma would have clobbered her when she was a kid for what Grandma thinks is so cute in her grandchildren. As for his brother and sister— Bea takes Byron in stride and Paul, of course, cannot understand it.

"We went to a support group, but only got platitudes about 'saving our Gay children'—nothing about saving *our* sanity. I suppose they meant well, but I felt like the oppressor because I questioned my son's life-style. If they could give their kids a 'straight' pill to turn them around, believe me, they would. I'm not ready for a Gay child on top of the other two."

Ann, Byron's mother, agreed with her husband. She told me:

"So if he became straight, he'd be only partly happy. Who has it all? I see marriage as the only norm. He could marry and take up a hobby to use up the stored energy, like racquetball. If Byron rejects our standards, we have the same option to reject his. I won't have him bringing those Gay people into my house or talking about his bizarre life-style in front of the family. I absolutely believe that he is acting out a grievance against us. Of that I'm convinced.

"In the weeks that have passed since he came out to us, I feel no more sanguine about it. No way. I feel that a parent may always withhold approval. I don't have to accept what is abhorrent to me. I have to be true to myself and my beliefs, no matter what demands are made on me. I know that some people consider homosexuality 'natural,' but I don't; any more than it's natural for Paul to be retarded and Bea to be epileptic.

"If we all get lucky and Byron changes his mind about being Gay, the fewer people who know the better. That's why I don't tell friends or family. Secondly, that mother-blame stuff would put me on the defensive. I don't fit into any of those suffocating-mother categories. Byron always had a certain amount of freedom and I'm not going to be the heavy in this. I have my own beliefs as to why Byron says he's Gay. I believe that he has been influenced by the proselytizing of Gay college friends—Gay hotlines at college, manned by Gays, are responsible for persuading a kid who's undecided about his sexuality that it's hurray for Gay. Another problem for me is that I notice an exhibitionism about his love affairs that never surfaced when he dated girls. I think he's trying to punish us by ramming his queer relationships down our throats."

CAROL AND CARL: "...now we're even closer"

Carol and Carl, a couple who invited me to interview them at their house one Sunday afternoon in a New Jersey suburb, are parents in their forties with four sons, aged eighteen, twenty, twenty-two, and twenty-four, and a ten-year-old daughter. The two younger boys came out almost simultaneously three years ago. These parents supported their Gay sons and encouraged the other children to do the same. They practically bristled with encouragement. It could not have been easy for them living as they do in a small, tight community. Even so, they have marshaled themselves to be acknowledged and accepted as a different kind of family. Carl says:

> "Carol and I both agree that we've always been close as a family, but now we're even closer. We talk about things we used to avoid. Now our boys talk to us about almost anything: our straight sons talk about their girlfriends, our Gay sons about their male friends, and our daughter about her problems. There is no self-consciousness; the younger boy will not necessarily seek out his Gay brother when he wants to discuss a problem—sexual or otherwise. He is perfectly comfortable talking about anything with either of his straight older brothers."

Carol says:

> "Two years ago, our older Gay son came out to his older brother, who then hinted about it to us. We approached him, and he admitted to us that he was Gay. As for the younger son, we actually pushed him into admission. He was acting troubled and withdrawn and we urged him to confide

in us. We were in couple therapy at the time, so our initial reaction was guilt. We believed our problems had driven the boys to homosexuality. Then we spoke to our therapist, who reminded us of how we always spoke lovingly of our children, and that we now know something else about them. We didn't, of course, notice anything drastically different about them, but it mattered. Their being Gay mattered very much. Our therapist suggested that we read *Society and the Healthy Homosexual*, which we did as well as other good pro-Gay literature—thirstily sponging up any information we could get. We went to a Parents of Gays group. It helped. Because we both came from a homophobic society, it was very difficult to accept the fact of two Gay sons. At first, we tried to see it as a passing problem. A phase. Months passed, however, and we realized that this was the indisputable truth. Two of our beloved sons were Gay to stay. We knew, though, that we would be there in every way to help them. We would be political activists and try to communicate our support to other parents."

Carl adds:

"We're closer and stronger than ever before. We need each other and we are very aware that the world is waiting out there to do the Gay kid in—if we let it. We are in an emotional karate position to hit back with everything we've got to protect our kids. At first Carol was reluctant to tell our friends and family. I was all for telling anyone and everyone. Now we would both tell the world. We're proud of our kids. They are great in school, terrific at sports and good to each other. We will not let them be judged on their sexuality alone."

MEL: "...I probably had a homosexual son"

Mel, a podiatrist who was referred to me by a friend at Fordham, is well into his seventies. His only child, Ian, now forty, is a dean in a New England college. Although Mel's wife died several years ago without realizing that her son was homosexual, Mel had suspected it since the boy was sixteen. Mel's eventual acceptance of Ian's homosexuality was conditional—as long as Ian was not "obvious." Ian has little choice in the manner in which his father chooses to recognize him, if he wants any kind of relationship with Mel. Meeting me near the library at Fordham, Mel told me:

"Ian was the only male dancer in his summer camp show, lifting the girls in the ballet that they performed for parents' visiting day. I was shocked, thinking that Ian looked effeminate and wondering why he would want to be the only fellow in the show. Ian, popular with both boys and girls, was never athletic. He majored in languages in college, for which he seemed to have a special gift. When he went out west for his Ph.D., he wrote that a male friend was coming with him and that they would be living together. I put this whole possibility of homosexuality in the back of my mind, but when he later got a position at this New England college and wrote that the same friend would be going with him, I had undercurrents of anger. I could not believe that I probably had a homosexual son.

"My nephew then approached me and, acting as go-between, told me that my fears were true: Ian was Gay—as they say nowadays. My nephew said that Ian was afraid that I would break off relations. He had seen me cut people off before and was afraid that it would happen to him, too. I *would* have disowned him, but a good friend of mine, acting as an intermediary, urged me to think about it. I was being pretty much of a schmuck, I guess, because I never stopped loving him. I decided at that time to go to Ian's school and suggest that we vacation together. Ian said fine. We went camping and never discussed the subject. I knew that he knew that I knew. I thought to myself, 'What would the world come to if we all were Gay?' Ian suggested that I read something by Gore Vidal on cloning, which I did, but it didn't change my mind. I felt and still do that the way to be is heterosexual.

"But Ian knows that I accept and love him. He happens—fortunately—to be quite lovable. Recently he and his friend made a tenth anniversary party to celebrate their years together and invited half the town. They certainly are loyal to each other and steady in a way too many heterosexuals today are not.

"I am grateful that Ian's not a swish. This helps me to mitigate his homosexuality. He lives a useful life and is highly regarded by his colleagues. He would come through for me if I needed him. I know it. Sure, he has subtle mannerisms, but they're not too obvious. He is a noted lecturer around the country. I am not ashamed of him. After all, I also have an antipathy to the blatant heterosexual who brags about his sexual conquests. I'll never have grandchildren. That would have been wonderful, and I admit I was in a blue funk over what I did to cause this. Just recently, I was going through some old letters from Ian's college days and other teenage memorabilia, and I came across a letter from a boy which indicated that the writer was homosexual and admired Ian for not 'playing the field as I did.' I then realized that Ian had been a practicing homosexual for a long time."

MINNA: "My psychic told me"

Minna, a gnarled, lined, old-country Greek woman in her late sixties, spoke in a Greek coffee shop near her home, of a psychic who pays her house calls and who blew the whistle on her son. Minna, who threw her son out of the house, is now weighing the advantages of having a caring, loving, live-in son, albeit Gay, compared to going it alone into old age. The importance of his sexual orientation seems to have diminished in the light of her need. Minna says:

"My psychic comes to the house every other week, and the last time I saw her she told me that my nineteen-year-old son Jon is a homosexual. She also said that he poses for the covers of male magazines and that I would see him on the cover of such a magazine if I went to the newsstand on the corner. I did go to look and there he was, half-naked, laughing and hugging another man.

"I went home and threw the magazine in his face. He threw it to the floor shouting that his modeling is what feeds us. I said that I would rather starve. He has moved out but still sends me a small check regularly. I don't know if I can get social security because I'm not a U.S. citizen. Anyway, now I don't care what Jon is. I am lonely and want him to come home again. Most of my family is dead or in Europe and I want my son back. I'm afraid to be alone in the apartment. I know now that Jon was a good son and that I've hurt him. How can I undo the harm? I'm so afraid to be alone."

DANA/KIRK: *"She was afraid we would cut her out of our will"*

Dana and Kirk, a distinguished-looking couple, active in community and church affairs in Scarsdale, New York, have three daughters—each "appropriately" married to ambitious corporate executives. The two older girls were absorbed in their new lives in a midwestern city, and each had two children. The youngest daughter, Dena, lived near her parents. Dana and Kirk were enjoying their "golden" years: comfortable retirement that offered a sturdy pension and income from holdings; golf; travel; and a social life at their country club. One day thirty-two-year-old Dena told her parents that she and her husband were planning a divorce. Stunned, the parents had seen this seven-year marriage as ideal. (Besides, there had never been a divorce in the family.) When they pressed Dena for a reason, she finally admitted that she had always had Lesbian feelings, but she felt that if she were married and conformed to the heterosexual world, she would overcome her strong feelings for women. It had not happened. Although she liked her husband, she felt she was denying herself and cheating him. She was simply playing a part and her husband didn't deserve that. She also confessed she had fallen in love with a female teacher in the school where they both taught and that they would go away together to start a new life. The other woman was divorced but had no children. Dana, shocked and mystified, says:

> "Dena has always been the most acquiescent and compliant of the three girls. She was never rebellious and always seemed to want the traditional: engagement party, bridal shower, church wedding. She even furnished her house the way ours

was furnished. It was as though what we held dear mattered to her, too. I even wondered why she wouldn't want to be more original when it came to decorating. Now I see that this was an attempt—like her marriage—to fall in line with us. But if she can't, she can't.

"If Dena has the guts to come out and say that she is in love with a woman, then I respect her feelings. We've had long talks about this and I believe that she knows who she is. If she picked this woman to love, then she must be special, because Dena is special. I intend to see her through any discomfort people may inflict on her."

Kirk, Dena's father, says:

"The two older girls have their own lives in a distant state. We only see them twice a year, if that much, and talk on the phone no more than once a month. Dena, on the other hand, has always been extremely close to us. In a family crisis, she has held out her hand to us. I will not tolerate any slander or unfair criticism of her. I must admit that although she is dainty and graceful, I wondered years ago about the intensity of a couple of her relationships with girlfriends. I would catch her gazing at them with such adoration that I wondered if sometimes this was not more than just chumminess. But when I saw the direction she chose—to marry and fit in with our community and life-style—I figured that she had outgrown all that.

"We make several trips a year and have told our daughters that if we died in a common accident that our estate would be split three ways among the three girls. Apparently Dena's sisters have approached her about our will, pointing out that since she is a declared Lesbian and will not be raising a family, her financial needs are less. They suggested she talk to us about relinquishing half of what we intend for her.

"Dena was extremely agitated about this request from her sisters. She wanted to know if her sisters were more equal than she was because they had husbands and children. She wanted to know if we intended to cut her out of our will.

"My insides ached for what she was going through and for what she kept hidden most of her life. I have since read a lot on homosexuality and I accept that it is happenstance that some children are inclined toward the same sex. I told her that her mother and I are not going to make life any harder by giving her less than she deserves. We're certainly not going to cut her out of our will."

HORACE: "So what did you get for Christmas—a tutu?"

Horace, a widower in his middle sixties, built up a thriving leather-goods business after starting as an office boy in the twenties and had lost his wife four years before our interview. Since her death, he had been plagued with an assortment of ills: cataracts, gallbladder and heart surgery. Until his recent illness, he had been estranged from his only son—Lou—for many years. Horace says:

"My son Lou is a character actor. He's not a star, but he has appeared so often in radio, TV and films that his face is familiar to many people. People stop him in the street to say that they know him but they're not sure from where.

"Ten years ago, when Lou told us that he was

Gay, his mother took it all right, but I saw red whenever they spoke on the phone or when Lou visited. It seemed like show business was no work for a real man. I had a going business and I wanted him in it with me. Father and son together. He refused and I took his refusal as a rejection of me and the business I had built up. I guess I was pretty much geared to having things my own way. I'm not proud of the way I was with both Lou and with my wife. I couldn't seem to control the meanness that overtook me at times. My idea of a joke when Lou was a little boy was to blow out the candles on his birthday cakes before he could. It would upset Lou and his mother. But I couldn't control either my tongue or my actions. I was like a big-bully kid. Maybe I was annoyed that Lou cried so easily. I wanted him tough, holding in his feelings the way I did—the way real men did.

"One day I fixed myself real good with my son. It was Christmas Day and Lou had brought a young man home. We were going to spend the day together, have dinner and then exchange gifts. I figured that Lou had felt that the holiday was a good time to spring this fellow on me because I would be soft and mellow. Maybe I wouldn't cause too many problems on Christmas Day.

"Meanwhile I was doing a slow burn about the whole scene. When it came time for the friend to open his gift, I sneered, 'So what is it—a tutu?' The three of them blanched. They were shocked. Then the boys headed for the door. Just took their coats and left without a word. My wife cried. That one remark caused a rift between us that never healed. I thought, 'Please come back, son.' But I never said it. I never said his name. Not for years and years until he called me when his mother was in the hospital. We sat silently next to each other at her funeral, not looking at each other, and afterward each going our separate ways.

"Lou and his young fellow were still together after almost ten years. That's longer than most of my divorced nieces and nephews. Then I got sick. One thing after another. They called. They came to see me in the hospital. Drove me home. Cared for me. Cooked for me. We finally talked. I still don't understand what he means by 'Gay' but I don't care what he means. I have my son back. A golden Gay son. I don't deserve to have him back. I was so rotten to him. But somehow it's okay now. We're getting to know each other from scratch. His friend is warming up to me more and more. I still have a family."

ALVIN: "Barney has broken our hearts"

Alvin and Annie, a couple whom I met while visiting Kenny and Sam, had already struggled with their son's homosexuality; they were now clasping him back to their breast along with his lover ever so tightly. Too tightly? Alvin says:

"Barney, our thirty-four-year-old son, just ran away from home with another man. He slipped stealthily out of the house one night about three weeks ago. In the note he left, he said that he was, is and always will be Gay. He and his lover have bought a condominium in Key West where they hope to live happily ever after. Barney has broken our hearts. We miss him dreadfully. We thought that we were a snug little family and did not need the company of the outside world. Some years ago, during the Vietnam War, we were agitating to get Barney a 4-F. Still, we were unprepared for what he did. He saw a psychiatrist to obtain a letter saying that he was Gay. When we told him over and over that such a letter would be forever on his record, he repeated stubbornly, 'I said I'm Gay, I said I'm Gay.' We were surprised at how easily Barney got this letter from the doctor, but now it all fits in. Last night when we called him, he said that we haven't lost a son, but have gained another son. We never thought that we would suddenly become parents to a man our age.

"We're thinking about retiring to Florida ourselves. Then we could be near the boys and be part of their everyday lives. We're going to call them to see if they want us to be near them. We miss our son so much."

MRS. G.: "We consider him a bright, healthy and loving young man"

Mr. and Mrs. G., a couple I met through another colleague at Fordham, were anxious to talk with me about their son. I visited them in their home in a New Jersey suburb. Mrs. G. says:

"We never had a homosexual in our family to our knowledge, but when our son revealed himself as one in a letter from college, we promptly sent him a telegram saying that we loved and supported him in any path he takes. We consider him a bright, healthy and loving young man—normal in every way. We are both independent-thinking people and did not and will not allow society, the media or the clergy to influence our love, admiration and acceptance of our son."

MAC: "I grabbed him by the neck...."

Mac, a tall, balding man, nicely dressed, appeared gentle and well mannered when he approached me at the downtown coffee shop where we had arranged to meet. I realized, as he began to speak, how his appearance covered up his cruel outlook and behavior. Mac said:

"I'm divorced and raised my son—if he is my son—to be a man. I took custody when I caught his bitch of a mother playing around—fucking anybody. So, I threw her out. I'm a traveling salesman and I came home one day early last year from the road. When I opened the door, I smelled tea rose perfume all over the house. I know what the stuff smells like because a woman I screw dunks herself in it. I hate it. I ran upstairs and there was my sixteen-year-old son, dressed in a ruffled skirt, made up and smelling like a whore and wafting around his room like some freaky fairy. I had suspected for some time that he was a loser like his bitch of a mother. I grabbed him by the neck, marched him down the stairs and into the street, which was filled with shoppers and neighbors. I paraded him in front of everybody for twenty minutes, yelling, 'Look what I got for a son.' Then I took off my belt and with the buckle beat him to the ground. No one stopped me or did anything. I locked the door of my house and told him that I was through with him. Let the shelter have him. I don't know where he is now and I don't care."

JANET: "The Lesbian women helped me to accept the facts"

Janet L., who answered my ad and asked me to meet her in the lobby of the public high school where she teaches social studies, is a married woman. Her son had come out to her and her husband when he was sixteen. Her Lesbian friends helped her to understand. Janet says:

"I have been working in a group composed mostly of Lesbian women, whom I like and respect. Nevertheless, finding out that a beloved son is Gay is not easy. The Lesbian women helped me to accept the facts. When I told my husband, he was hurt and it was difficult to accept, but what could he do? However, he insisted that we keep it secret and when I mentioned it at our marriage encounter group, he almost blew his mind. When our son came out to us he was sixteen and we considered him adult enough to know his own mind. I have made myself available to counsel other people who have Gay children. The world will only progress as we help each other through it."

THE LETTERS

EVAN: "This is family business—immediate family"

Evan wrote me a long letter after my ad appeared in the newspaper. His immediate problem was not a reaction to his son Archer's recent coming out, but to

Archer's insistence on bringing a male date to a family wedding with the full intention of dancing with his mate. Evan's tirade was motivated by the feeling that Archer should be selective in where and to whom he displayed overt Gay orientation. Certainly Evan had some rights and perhaps Archer was insistent on being exhibitionistic at an inappropriate place. Certainly the bride and bridegroom had some rights to be the main attraction on their special day. If Evan did not attend the wedding, Archer would ultimately feel guilty and the conflict would worsen. The hostility that Archer felt in wanting to make a public statement was misplaced; the terrain, unsuitable. Evan and Archer, who was seventeen, had been at each other's throats for weeks. Says Evan:

"My wife sides with Archer. She is Italian, and her side of the family is making the wedding. She won't see that this part of the family is forties vintage; they waltz, they foxtrot, they dip. Remember dips? Can you see their reaction when my kid dips his partner? I'm going to get whiplash looking the other way. Archer is unpredictable. He doesn't care. He always did what he wanted to do to get attention. He tells his mother everything. So I ask her, 'Will they tango? Will they dance cheek to cheek?' I insist that they don't hold hands or dance at that wedding. What am I supposed to do? Get up at the mike and explain to seventy-five people that Archer is Gay? This is family business—the immediate family. Not the cousins and the uncles and the aunts. They don't have to know our private stuff. I don't want whispers and whistles at an old-fashioned family wedding."

DIANA: "I must crawl before I walk"

Diana, a forty-seven-year-old mother of three daughters, was terrified to challenge her husband when it came to the defense of her Gay daughter. Diana wrote:

"My youngest daughter, Meg, twenty-four years old, has left her husband to move in with her female lover. She has a beautiful little girl of four. Her husband swears he is going to fight her in court and take the child away from her. He already has another woman who has a child of her own. Meg says she cannot bear for this to happen. She cries all the time. I am in fear of losing touch with my only grandchild and in fear of my husband finding out. He is a heavy drinker and has a terrible temper.

"I'm afraid of violence. He has raised his hands to all of us before. The other daughters live nearby. They know that their sister is a Lesbian, but my husband doesn't know. It is only a matter of time before he finds out. I am terrified of how he'll react. He will blame me.

"Lesbianism goes against my grain. I can't see women together. Not that male-female relationships are so great, but we have to put up with men. They bring home the money and have the say.

"Meg says no matter how rotten her father has behaved, I never stood up for her. But I need time. I have to talk to my priest. I have to crawl before I can walk."

EVE: "He could be more"

Eve, a retired federal employee in her fifties, was—not surprisingly—bitter: in the past year, her parents had been killed in an automobile accident; her divorce had become final; she had had a mastectomy; and Ernie, her twenty-one-year-old son, had come out to her as Gay. Eve, extremely homophobic, treated Ernie as though he had a terminal illness. Her expectations were unrealistic, considering she had never evinced much interest in higher learning herself. Because she made him feel unworthy, he would probably drift irrevocably out of her life. Eve says:

> "Ernie picked a fine time to tell me—on my birthday. Becoming fifty wasn't traumatic enough? My husband and I adopted him when he was two, hoping a child would help our marriage. It didn't. We got him through less-than-legal Canadian sources, and we always suspected he was part Indian. My husband, who obviously had no fathering skills, fought with Ernie constantly. When he was really angry he would threaten, 'I'll take away your tomahawk,' nastily taunting Ernie about having Indian blood.
>
> "When Ernie came out of the closet, my husband, glad of an excuse to dump the boy, became so enraged that he said he never wanted to see him again. Ernie's life centers around being Gay. That's it. He is a bartender in a Gay bar. His friends are all Gay. He only reads Gay newspapers and magazines. My pain is that he won't amount to much more. He acts as though being Gay is a career.
>
> "Ernie didn't do well in school, but I feel that the good salary and tips are going to destroy what little ambition he has. I feel demeaned that my son works in a bar for tips. I'm too ashamed to tell even the person closest to me, my sister, or anyone else that he is Gay. People would have one more thing on me, and I don't need that. Ernie is

taking a place in the Village next week. The men in my life leave me en masse. I shouldn't have retired. Now I don't know what to do with myself."

KATYA: "He was always drawing penises"

Katya and her husband, both translators employed by the United Nations, are Dutch. Hendrik, their twenty-year-old son, had come out in a unique way. He had left an original book of cartoons—his own artwork—on his mother's dressing table. Through her writing, I felt that Katya had an easygoing kind of personality, and wrote that her family seemed to communicate whole-heartedly without the need of words. Katya wrote:

"At first I thought that Hendrik was just simply a penis-obsessed cartoonist. Even as a child, he was always drawing penises. When he doodled, he would draw these long wiggly traveling things with sweet little faces. The eyebrows would be surprised, the eyes like wide marbles and always the funny smile. The penis would explore, look and act friendly.

"Some of the drawings would show children at their desks; some would show teacher at the blackboard or at the desk. The penis would stop and look up her skirt or down the top of her blouse. From the length and territory covered, one had the impression that the penis was yards and yards long.

"Sometimes it would slither through a key-hole and visit another classroom. The last two years all of the cartoons showed it stopping to gaze at a handsome boy student. The boy student would be shown to gaze back, face propped up on elbows.

"Hendrik is in college now. For the last weeks, the dated cartoons show the snakelike penis stopping at every desk, which is always occupied by the same boy. The boy has a noticeable erection although fully clothed. From this, I think my boy is Gay. Last week he invited a young man for dinner to our apartment. I recognized him as the face in the cartoons.

"We have never needed to talk about this. Hendrik knows that I looked at his cartoon book. I have shown it to my husband who says that he hopes our son will pick nice people to love. I welcome his friends and I hope he will have a good life."

ALICE: "Our nineteen-year-old son was lost to us from AIDS*...."

"Alice" answered my ad by writing a five-page letter from which I excerpt the most poignant paragraph. "Alice" writes:

"We are not letter-writing people, but we have to say this because we know you counsel parents of homosexual children. Our nineteen-year-old son was lost to us from AIDS in March. We never even knew that he was Gay. When we heard from the hospital, he was almost finished. We knew that he was never at his apartment at night.

---

*If three-fourths of all AIDS victims are Gay men, it would seem logical to counsel selectivity and discretion in sexual conduct. Perhaps if parents nag and nudge their Gay sons to be extremely selective and cautious, the sons might take heed, feeling reassured that their parents care very much what happens to them. The problem of AIDS can be related to the problem of syphilis, which was regarded as a sinister incurable killer until finally a cure was discovered. Syphilis is indiscriminate, striking both homosexual and heterosexual alike. Our concern must be with cure and prevention rather then with moral judgment.

Whenever we called, he was out. Many times early in the morning, he was out. We're not saying that this is God's wrath (as we read in some church papers), but we are saying that we know how much venereal disease there is in this country—and now there's this AIDS. We think that the papers and television could come right out and say that indiscriminate sex kills. We would not have turned away from our son if he had told us what he was. Now it's too late. Tell other parents of these kids to talk to them about knowing who they go with."

ANITA: "We worry that he will be hurt in his profession"

"My son, who only went around with boys, kept leaving signals around the house: Gay newspapers, articles about Gay people, matches from Gay bars and restaurants. I eventually got the message. My husband did, too, but neither one of us admitted it to the other. When we confronted our son separately, he insisted that we all three sit down together and talk about it. After two years, we are finally facing the reality. Our son, who is in graduate school, is still living at home. We worry that he will be hurt in his profession."

MR. X.: "In my deepest heart, I wish him dead"

"I am sixty years old, and I won't permit my son to bring his lover to my house. I don't want to completely lose him, but I can't compromise my ideals. In my deepest heart, I wish him dead. I've been to a psychiatrist, but I still can't cope with this."

MRS. JONES: "...it is God's will"

"I believe that it was St. Augustine who said, 'If evil is caused by the flesh, how explain the wickedness of the devil who has no flesh?' Our son has not a wicked bone in his body. If this is the way of his flesh, then it is God's will. The devil played no part."

MRS. H.: "I accept his Gayness and support him"

"When my son came out to me at the age of seventeen, I was concerned that he was not ready to make such a decision. I threatened his twenty-six-year-old lover with arrest if he didn't leave my minor child alone. This, in retrospect, is amusing, *considering that I, too, am Gay.* I have been seeing another woman for the past few years quite openly. Our relationship evolved in a loving and natural way and I did talk to my son about it. He seemed unperturbed."

"I accept his Gayness and support him. Since he is now at college and we see less of each other, our relationship is changing from one of mother and son to that of friends. He is a talented person who I respect and admire.

"My son's father died when he was five. He had loved his father dearly. He was a special boy, loving movies, costuming and painting. His male peers played too roughly for his taste. As an artist myself, I believe that I influenced my son to discover his own artistic talents. He wanted to be like me. My younger boy, now fifteen, on the other hand, was a 'normal' boy, even without a male role model—this makes one wonder whether the cause of my older son's Gayness is genetic.

"Male homosexuality seems far different from Lesbianism. I worry about my son becoming involved with many sexual partners and being hurt by the experiences. That is my big concern. I fear that he will be devastated by a casual life. I feel that it doesn't matter who one loves, but *that* one loves."

MRS. A.: "...He might be bisexual...."

Mrs. A. wrote that she and her husband were split about her only son's homosexuality: that she accepted it at once when he came out to her at twenty-five years of age. She said that her husband took the "see a psychiatrist" route but that she asked her son to leave himself open to other options—to continue to see women and not to take any infatuation with another male as definitive of Gayness. She felt strongly that because of his closeness with girls in the past that he might be bisexual depending upon who attracted him at the moment.

MR. M.: "...I'm fighting with my family...."

"I am a closet parent, yet I find that I'm fighting with my family and friends every time they say something homophobic. I jump on them and tell them they are bigots, but I haven't had the guts to come right out and say that my daughter, a real doll, who my wife and I love no matter who she loves or what she calls sex, is a Lesbian.

"We both like and accept her girlfriend whom she calls 'lover.' They are both as cute as buttons and we go everywhere together. I like running around with my beautiful harem. But, when people ask why the hell am I defending Gays, I clam up. I can't say that I have a homosexual daughter and that she has rights. I just fight. My kid doesn't care who I tell, but I find that I can't just blurt it out! I sent a check to the Gay Task Force anonymously. The words just won't come out when I'm confronted with the 'What's it to you guys?'"

MR. B.: "...I have a great kid who happens to be Gay"

Mr. B., who wrote that he finds himself laughing at Gay jokes at parties along with the others, adds:

"I am with my nineteen-year-old Gay son all the way. But when I'm with friends, I listen to the usual anti-Gay jokes. I am afraid to tell them to shut their stupid mouths—that I have a great kid who happens to be Gay. Instead, I take another drink and laugh along with them. I hate my cowardice because I'm guilty of perpetuating contempt for Gay people every time I laugh at a snide remark. Yet, I can't say anything. I even kept quiet at a cocktail party when a medical doctor was spewing out anti-Gay hatred with a vehemence that shocked me. The man said that he would be happy to perform vasectomies 'on the whole lot of them,' and I said nothing, while inside my heart was breaking and I wanted to break his balls. I hate that I'm no help to my son. At home, with the immediate family, my wife and two daughters, we hold our boy close. Maybe later I'll talk out, but it's only four months since I found out."

MRS. C.: "We attend church...often with my daughter's lover"

"When my eighteen-year-old daughter told me that she was Gay, I went through the usual soul-searching and wound up with my minister. We are Presbyterians. He told me that he himself was homosexual and that the church officials knew it but the congregation did not. He was able to stay on as minister because of a grandfather clause which granted religious asylum to a known existing homosexual minister. But at this time, new seminarians who admitted that they were homosexual were denied ordination.

"My minister told me that the prohibitions against homosexuality which seem clear in the Bible were written in a particular historical context. It was believed two thousand years ago that people were homosexual by choice, not condition, and were knowingly acting in a manner unnatural to them and therefore unnatural to their own God-given nature. The religionists also saw homosexuality as unnatural to them—therefore unnatural, period. In the light of modern knowledge, this does not hold true.

"I was tremendously relieved to hear him point this out, because my deepest concern was that my girl was going against God and church. His ideas make sense to me. We attend church as a family, often with my daughter's lover, and feel good and right about it. But we dare not say anything to anyone about their being homosexual. We just know in our hearts that God wants us in his hearts, too."

MRS. F.: "We are Jewish and my son's lover was not"

"My son and his lover actually went through a wedding ceremony conducted by a rabbi. Invalid though it might be, they consider themselves married. My family has known for years that my son is Gay. They were noncommittal but objected strenuously to the term 'lover,' saying that it indicated sexuality. Anyway, we are Jewish and my son's lover was not. Would you believe that he converted? He has gone through all the learning and now considers himself Jewish. This is more than a former girlfriend of my son's was willing to do.

"I don't believe that this rabbi is in much favor with the synagogues; neither is the ceremony he elected to preside over for us. I made a small party later in my home, where the ceremony took place, and no one in the family refused to come. Maybe they wanted something to snicker about. I have signed over my house to the couple and am moving to a studio apartment. In celebration, my son carried his groom over the threshold to emphasize their new beginning—no mean feat because that groom weighs 200 pounds. I am glad that my son has someone to care for him and that he won't be alone in life without love as I am. I won't be around long, though. I have terminal cancer."

MR. AND MRS. E.: "...we march in the Gay parade..."

"After both our son and daughter came out to us as Gay, we found our way into a group that urged us to become politically active for Gay rights. Our kids call us the Lone Rangers, cheering us on whenever we march in the Gay parade or vocally campaign for Gay rights."

MRS. Z.: "I told him to keep it under his hat..."

"My son came out to us last year. I told him to keep it under his hat and not let anyone else know. At an Elks' dinner dance, he sat with us, very grumpy because we forbade him to bring a male date. He pointed to several of the women who were dancing together and demanded to know why it was acceptable for *them* to cavort around the dance floor together—but not for him. We told him that when a woman has to dance with another woman, it means that she cannot find an escort to be her dance partner, but when two men dance together it means only that they're Gay."

THE QUESTIONNAIRES

MICHAEL M.: "It is an honor to have my son in our family"

"I am seething. Some religious leaders and other self-styled leaders like Bryant and Falwell are the 'immoral' ones because they preach love and hatred in the same breath. This world has seen its share of wars, starvation, plagues, cruelty, gas chambers and more, mostly perpetrated by the non-Gay world. Yet the demagogues need a scape-goat, the homosexual. Most of the Gays I have met, like my own son, are decent, law-abiding human beings: taxpayers; voters; and, aside from their sexual orientation, no different in their desires and needs from the likes of us. It is an honor to have my son in our family, and if 'family' is the strength of our country, I'll hold mine high up in pride."

PAULINE N.: "The neighbors must have heard our screams..."

"Our son ran and hid every time he heard an off-color word or a dirty joke. He blushed when we spoke to him. He was really inordinately shy. One night, when he was fifteen, we went to the movies, leaving him and a male schoolmate alone to supposedly do homework together. We didn't like the film and decided to return home early. There they were, entangled like a pretzel, mouthings going like motors, clothes all over the living room. The neighbors must have heard our screams for blocks. We chased him around the house for an hour with a hanger—the only thing we could get our hands on fast. The other boy hurried home. Of course, we couldn't catch him, but when he finally gave up and sat down breathless and exhausted, our shrinking violet came out to us. What could we do or say? He is still prudish. We still cannot use profanity in front of him. His young lover lives with us while they are both still in college. They are very prissy, nonhumorous young men, but that's the way it is."

SALLY J.: "...he won't be permitted to realize his potential"

"My ex-husband doesn't know about our son because my son and I decided that he wasn't emotionally equipped to handle it. I went to our family doctor, who knew absolutely nothing about the subject. I found myself explaining to him the little I knew. When my son realized that I was not about to throw the book at him for his 'transgressions,' he melted down and became my friend once more—after a period of prolonged hostility. We're closer than ever now. However, I fear that because he is Gay, he won't be permitted to realize his potential in a homophobic society."

PAT: "...his homosexuality is not my business"

"I am Hispanic, and I don't care much that my son, Tony, is Gay. As long as he keeps contributing money to the house, what he does with his time is his own business. There are smaller children in my family. I need his financial help—he is the oldest. I have no man here. As long as he gives, and I hope he continues to give, his homosexuality is not my business. I am not so different from many other Hispanic people in my thinking. My son works, makes money and is the head of the house. What he says goes. He is good to his younger brothers and sisters. What do I care about Gayness—we all need him."

LOU: "For myself, I'm a tit man. Empty cups turn me off"

"I do not have a problem that my son Rick is Gay. But I was curious about how Gay men found each other and what turned them on. For myself, I'm a tit man. Empty cups turn me off. Rick has had the same lover, Ike, for the last year. When I asked Rick about what it was that made him pick out this particular guy, Rick told me they had met on a nude beach in San Diego and that Ike was lying facedown on the sand. 'Pop,' said Rick, 'when Ike stood up, Christ, what a gigantic hole he left in the sand.' So I found out just what it was that my son found so attractive in Ike."

SONIA: "I am so miserable that I haven't slept in weeks"

"My daughter is now living with a woman who left her husband of twenty-five years and is filing for divorce. This woman has two grown daughters of her own, one of whom is pregnant. My daughter is only twenty. According to my daughter, neither has ever had a Lesbian affair before, but they steadfastly maintain they are in love. When I hear my daughter use the term 'lover,' I get sick. The other woman is older than I am. Can you imagine how I feel? Her husband called me and accused me of letting my daughter ruin his marriage. He blames everything on my daughter. I am terrified that he will do something about the threats he is making. I am ashamed to go to the police because this is a small upstate community, and I just think that the husband is hysterical, as who wouldn't be. My husband says that until my daughter leaves this woman, she many not enter our house.

"The woman's daughters will not talk to her or see her. Our minister thinks that the two of them should either break up or leave the community. I am so miserable that I haven't slept in weeks. Our lives had been so good before this. Now we are all torn up."

MR. AND MRS. Y.: "...a psychiatrist suggested electric shock therapy to cure him"

"He kept the rope in his bedroom, playing with it or making Boy Scout knots. Once, when he was twelve years old, we threw the rope out, but soon another rope appeared in his room. When we asked him why he kept the rope near him, he replied there was no place for him in this world and that he might someday need it. Naturally we took him to a psychiatrist, who suggested electric shock therapy to 'cure' him of his possible homosexuality. We refused. We thought this 'treatment' too drastic. Our son had admitted to his attraction to boys and, believing his feelings were unnatural, felt moody and despondent. We assured him it was unnatural and therefore he *would* outgrow it.

"When he reached eighteen, however, he fell madly in love with his piano teacher. The love affair was short-lived, mostly because of our interference. When his teacher won a scholarship and moved to another town, our son withdrew into himself, refusing to talk to anyone. A month later, when he returned from school, he hanged himself in our recreation room, writing in a note that he had told us that there was no place for people like him in this world. Now our twenty-year-old daughter has told us she is a Lesbian and wants to have a child. She has arranged for artificial insemination by a man who is willing to sign away his rights to the child. Our daughter has our blessing to go for whatever she wants. We failed our son; we will not fail our daughter."

MR. AND MRS. D.: "...he was humiliated by our evangelism..."

"When our son came out to us, we went through all the stages of shock, bewilderment, concern. Then we found a support group, and we got rid of a lot of passion against our son's homosexuality. We transferred our anger to the outside world and its rulings against Gay people. We're using our energy to try to change discriminating laws against Gays. We've become gung-ho about it and allowed it to take over our lives. Our son then left town. He left a note saying that he was humiliated by our evangelism and the resulting publicity. He accused us of being self-serving, saying that he had a right to privacy. We are now in group therapy, and although we are still committed to activism for Gay rights, we act with more discretion. Our son is not as angry as we are about the discrimination around him and other Gay people, but now allows that although we are diligent about our political activities, we are not blatant. Our son is still out west, but we are friends again."

MRS. I.: "...prostitution frankly repelled..."

Mrs. I. sent me back my questionnaire with a full-page article enclosed which had appeared in a

California newspaper in the late seventies. This woman described how she learned that her son was Gay. She was frightened that her fifteen-year-old youngest boy had not yet returned home and it was the early hours of the morning. When the police finally called, she was almost ready for anything. At the station, she was taken to the holding room where she saw a tired-looking elderly man in drag, some women of the night and her son, wearing a mask of huge dark glasses. He saw her, took off the glasses, and she realized that he wore heavy eye makeup. He had been picked up for being out past curfew and for soliciting men. This woman, a divorcee, was consumed with shock and guilt. Her son was hospitalized for three months, during which time she was required to attend therapy with him. She developed an inner rage against the patronizing psychiatrist in charge. "He was no help. My heart told me that he is still my son and if he is happy in this life-style, then I must be happy for him and just love him. My love helped him to change from his dangerous life-style."

Mrs. I. wrote that the "too much mother and not enough father" claim by certain doctors is immaterial. Her other four children are not Gay. She refused to allow societal taboos to influence her feelings about her Gay son. She has initiated a local self-help group, accompanies her son to a Gay bar occasionally and exchanges confidences with his Gay friends, who are grateful for the opportunity to talk to an accepting parent. I heard from Mrs. I again several months later. She wrote that because of her interest and support and acceptance of her son's homosexuality—despite the prostitution, which "frankly" repelled her—his self-esteem had risen to the point where he no longer hangs out in Gay bars, has given up prostitution and has been able to take a few night courses. He intends, she writes, to enroll in a local college full-time.

MR. K.: "I say the cop was a crazed Gay-hater..."

"Four years ago, our son, aged eighteen, was stalked in the park in Florida by a cop. The police story was that he was loitering for purposes of prostitution and robbery. He was supposed to have approached the cop and invited him up to a nearby hotel room, having settled on a price. Five dollars. He was supposed to have lunged at the cop, going for the genitals. The cop said that he flashed a badge and that my son flashed a knife, a switchblade. They fought and my son was killed. We got a call in New York to come down for the body. If all of this was true, why was our kid carved like a turkey? His back was a mass of crisscrosses. The cop in question had a heart attack two weeks later and was retired. We never could get anywhere with any answers. My son was slow. He didn't have the sense to ask for money. He didn't have the sense to suggest a hotel. He had an IQ of eighty. I say that the cop was a crazed Gay-hater or sadist. And he got away with it. With only a heart attack and a pension. Our son never had a knife. Especially a switchblade. Sure, he used to look for boys. But he never hurt anyone. That Bryant witch and her mob helped kill him. She spread enough hate to kill lots of kids. Gave the crazies an excuse to witch hunt. We overheard a detective at the morgue say that our kid's death was no great loss. This is probably not the kind of story you are looking for, but now we are the living dead. There are probably lots of parents like us, who lost our kids to the 'law.' And what can we do? What can we prove?"

NORMA: "My marriage is threatened because of my husband's intolerance"

"I heard you on a radio program where you likened the difference of E.T. to the difference of being Gay.

"The society at large threatened E.T.'s very existence, but children who had not yet caught up with prejudice against different kinds of being befriended E.T.

"I'm reminded of my husband's rejection of my son, who is Gay. But my thirteen-year-old daughter remains loyal to her brother. She sees the fine person that he is and stands up for him. My marriage is threatened because of my husband's intolerance. Could he be so violently anti-Gay because he himself has leanings? From the minuscule interest my husband has shown in our sex life, I look at him askance."

BRETTA: "That's a beautiful son"

Bretta, a sixty-year-old woman who has marched in the parades with the Parents of Gays, is open about her identity as the mother of a Gay son. Bretta wrote:

"My son Gerard became sure of his homosexuality when his father was hospitalized with terminal leukemia. I had twenty-four-hour access to my husband and slept in the hospital four nights a week. When Gerard told me he was Gay three weeks after my husband died, I asked how long he had known. He told me he knew for certain just before his father became ill but he wasn't ready to tell us then. He said that after his father became ill he didn't think that under these conditions it was right to tell him. I was so involved in my husband's care that he didn't wish to burden me. That's a beautiful son."

• • •

Guilt was the pervading attitude. Husbands and wives tossed The Problem back and forth to each other like a hot potato. Often a mother or father would do as I had done—probe way back in time to pinpoint what he or she had done to "turn the child Gay."

All the parents that contacted me were relieved to be able to talk or write to someone who knew exactly what they were feeling. Many parents had experienced feelings similar to mine: the sense of loss, not unlike mourning. They were trying to work through the stages of burying the former image of their son or daughter, then reconstructing a new image. Often conflict arose between Gay children and their parents because the children demanded instant acceptance. The parents would complain—rightly so—that the child had lived with this knowledge for many years, but they, the parents, needed time to assimilate the news. Some parents had reached a stage of resolution; they realized they needed to educate themselves about the unfamiliar and frightening Gay world. Those who reached a point of acceptance (or resignation), declared that although life would present difficulties for their children, they were there for them. Some began to consider the political posture of Gay rights and others questioned— and even challenged—the precepts of their religion's intolerance toward homosexuality. Very few parents were *totally* rejecting. After all, if their antipathy and revulsion were frozen solid, why would they want to discuss it at all? After a while, I began to see a pattern, and I noted four prevailing attitudes among the parents with whom I connected:

1. Apparent Acceptance
The family tried *too* hard and was really uncomfort-

able in the presence of physical affection displayed between their Gay sons or daughters and lovers. However, they carried on with splendid bravado in their social milieu and in front of their Gay children.

2. Conditional Acceptance
The family says, "Okay, you're Gay. But let's keep it our little secret. We don't have to tell anyone, and, for God's sake, don't bring your strange friends home."

3. Avoidance Acceptance
The subject is not mentioned again; the life-style is not discussed again; the friends or lovers are treated as guests (or the lover is treated as a "friend").

4. Acceptance
The family has gotten used to the idea. They have allowed themselves to grow and to accept diversity.

Whatever the degree of acceptance, my contacts with these parents were fruitful in that they—and I—had the comfort of sharing. Now we knew we were not alone. It also became obvious that in many cases homosexuality was only *one* source of conflict between parents and children. Differences in attitudes on the use of drugs, styles of dress, respect toward elders—and other attitudes that traditionally aggravate the generations—fueled the conflicts. But most important to me was that this experience directed me toward specializing in work with families of Gays. I saw the need. I saw the gap. I believed this was the area where I was most equipped and ready to apply what I had learned through therapy, reading and contact with parents. I knew now that—

- the Kinsey Institute believes there is a deep-seated predisposition to homosexuality;

- parents may take a deep breath and expel their guilt feelings about responsibility for their children's homosexuality;

- there are some stereotypes, but hordes of Gay men and women do not correspond to hackneyed clichés;

- the Gay person yearns for the same warmth, love and family embrace that so many non-Gay people take for granted;

- many families of Gays want to educate themselves and to understand more about their Gay children so that these children may more comfortably fit into the family; and

- with family support and loyalty, the Gay person may realize success in life—that with the family standing behind the Gay son or daughter, the barriers may be lowered.

Most of the parental reactions were a result of religious and societal attitudes that have flourished unquestioned for too long. Now that homosexuality has touched on the lives of these parents, they are forced to take another look at old shibboleths. Why should ancient, musty writings turn us against our own children? Writings that approved the stoning to death of adulterers and inquisitions that resulted in torture and death for thousands. In this—the twentieth century—is it not time for straight parents and Gay children to progress toward love and understanding of each other? Does the child hurt anyone by being himself or herself with another consenting adult? Isn't morality a matter of conscience? Parents asked themselves these questions and plodded with difficulty toward coming to terms. Some made it. Others did not. Some did not even try. But those parents who made it through to varying degrees of understanding of their Gay children know the rewards of building and seeing that building take shape. They have not lost their Gay children. But what of the children who were reviled and rejected—what did they say?

What the Children Said

Childhood is only the beautiful and happy time
in contemplation and retrospect; to the child
it is full of deep sorrow, the meaning
of which is unknown.

—George Eliot, *George Eliot's Family Life and Letters*

I met them everywhere: at Gay parties, in the course of my practice, at support group meetings, in churches and temples, at college clubs, on social occasions, through Kenny and his friends and through my own friends who were mostly unaware that their children were Gay.

Some children were bitterly angry and unforgiving toward their families; some were cynical; some contemptuous when their families expected them to play a conventional role. Some—too few—enjoyed and appreciated acceptance and reassurance in various degrees of familial love.

But of these Gay children who had finally revealed themselves to their families all had served a long term alone with their self-knowledge.

WANDA: "I ducked the bouquets"

Wanda, a pretty twenty-nine-year-old quite secure in her Lesbianism, was an upstate New York WASP. She knew that in Daddy's eyes she could do no wrong and treats her rather conventional mother with affectionate tolerance. She obviously cares very much about family—not missing the celebrations and carrying her little secret tongue-in-cheek. I have no doubt that when she falls in love she will announce it to all and sundry and ask Daddy to give her away.

"It was a secret between my dad and me. I told him I was Gay nine years ago and he said, 'So what? You'll always be my little girl no matter how you do you-know-what. If you run into trouble, just yell and I'll come running to help—just as always.' I felt reassured that he didn't kick up his heels about my Gayness, but I also felt he didn't understand what the implications were. I told him I had just realized how much I loved the girl I roomed with at Vassar and that she loved me. We planned to buy a house upstate, open a crafts shop in the Berkshire area and live happily ever after. I'm sure my dad understood nothing about what I tried to convey. However, he nodded agreeably. The 'trouble' he had in mind was probably police busts in the bars or maybe he thought I would be in a girls' house of prostitution.

"Mom—old-fashioned, traditional, limited—was a different story. She was forever taking my grandmother's wedding dress out of mothballs and dangling it in front of me. The problem is the weddings. I have eight girl cousins who are marrying like crazy. And, they have been cornering me into being maid of honor, probably because they see that I have no interest in dating guys. I was a challenge. Not only am I marching every month in pastel bridal processions, but they throw the goddamned bouquet at me. When the bride winds up to serve me up her nosegay, I hunch my head into my collarbone, praying that she'll miss. If any one of those bouquets ever lands on me, I'm afraid that it could be some kind of voodoo and I might actually end up married."

EDWIN: "Father was a female"

Edwin, a twenty-seven-year-old bank teller, told me about his twelfth birthday—the day he found out that "Lem," his "stepfather," was actually Emma—his mother's female lover of eleven years. The shocking exposure of his "stepfather" has left scar tissue that will not go away, plus the feeling of being "outside" of society—outside of his mother's love. The damage done to this young man was unconscionable. At present he is trying to work through his problems in therapy:

"Mom was a dressmaker, unmarried when I was born—the year before she met Emma. We lived in a small, isolated mountain resort near the Canadian border, a couple of miles from the village. Winter usually showed up in early fall when the town had emptied itself of the tourists and residents braced for the long, dark and freezing months. Emma, on vacation, had met Mom when she brought her some clothes for alterations. Mom had told me when I was seven that my father was connected with the church and would never recognize me, so he was of no importance. It would only cause trouble for everyone—I'm sure they knew anyway. I accepted what Mom said—accepted that the 'Lem' who lived with us was Mom's 'husband.' From about the time I was eight years old, I realized I was Gay and different. I knew when I was young that I didn't have too many choices in life and that I would have to make do. To me, Emma was a guy, and I was happy to have an acting father. I was stupid and unobserving, of course, and I realize now that I had the naivete of the country hick.

"But 'Lem' could have fooled lots of people. She was 'butch': heavyset, muscular, and she loped when she walked. Her mode of dress, of course, was masculine, and her voice had the gravelly croak of the two-pack-a-day smoker. Anyway, where could I make comparisons? She treated me well and even helped with my homework. She was around a lot because she was doing some kind of mail-order work at home. I never loved her—him—but then I never dared love anyone. Even now. They could turn out to be someone else.

"The night that ended it all was when they were boozing it up all day. By nightfall, they were mean, angry and screaming: Mom, in long flannel nightgown; Emma, in striped flannel pajamas. Mom picked up the purple passion plant, their private joke—and swung it at Emma, whose left nipple gushed blood. Her breast itself was small, and I had seen it so many times that its exposure was not new to me. What was unusual was when 'Lem' screeched hysterically that 'he' was ripped open. Enraged and in pain, she tore off the already shredded pajamas. I saw pubic hair and *nothing else protruding*. Dumb as I was, I knew that something should have been sprouting from between those legs. I must have gone into a state of catalepsy for a few hours after that. When I came to, Emma had gone, and Mom, sobbing at the stove, was stirring soup. She looked up, saw me staring and came over to tell me her 'story.' How could she have possibly taken in such a dykey woman? Wasn't her reputation bad enough already? The community would have taken custody of me away from her. Begging me to understand, she told me that she did it for me. She told me that women love each other in a deeper, sexier and more lasting way than men love women.

"I remember that I glanced over at the empty bedroom. Mom—noticing—defended her behavior by saying, 'Look how long it lasted.' She insisted that the good caring years together were more than my father or any other man, for that matter, had offered her. She never did seem to think about what the charade had done to me. She was not very smart or educated. Years later, when I told her I was having affairs with young men, she threw me out."

JACOB: "My family sat shiva for me"

Jacob, a thirty-four-year-old dry cleaner, spoke coolly, but the bitterness underneath surfaced as he told his story:

"I won big in a lottery, but don't bother envying me. It hasn't helped me in the world or with my family. My parents were both born in Poland and fled to the United States during the Hitler era. They were fanatically religious Jews who sent me to the Yeshiva when I was very young. My life consisted of Talmudic studies. My childhood was constricted. Choked. My little world was surrounded by family constantly recounting Holocaust atrocities.

I had difficulty in swallowing food and was very skinny.

"It is myth that all Jews are kind to children. The rabbi was cruel. He trounced us with a yard-stick for the slightest infraction. My parents always backed him up saying that if he beat me, then I did something to deserve it. They were never on my side even before they found out that I was Gay.

"I told them twelve years ago. I still have a bare spot on my scalp where my father flew at me and yanked out a tuft of hair. They sat shiva for me. Jews do this when they mourn their dead. When my mother died two years ago, my sister called—going against my father—to tell me. At the funeral, no one spoke to me.

"It has taken years of therapy to help me to see my own self-worth. I see a Gay therapist. I used to see a straight one who wanted only to 'cure' me. When I won the lottery, guess who called me for money to help rebuild his vandalized temple? You got it. I told Pop that since I was no longer among the living and if he took money from a ghost, the temple would be forever haunted."

CARLOTTA: "I had to eat at a separate table for two years"

Carlotta was another victim of parental abuse. Her Lesbianism was only another excuse for these parents to vent their sadism. They would rather have seen her a battered wife than brimming with joy in the arms of a loving woman. Carlotta was Castilian Spanish, and her family had emigrated to the United States when she was four. At an all-girls' Catholic school, she met and fell in love with Lucia:

"My parents were morose and somber. I don't recall laughter or light, kindly talk at home; and my brother, the family prince, was as bad. He slept in the second bedroom while I slept on two overstuffed chairs pushed together in the living room. When I was sixteen, I fell in love with Lucia, a beautiful girl in one of my classes. We dreamed and talked together. We planned to start a home together when we got older. We used to meet in the park. Our need was so great we couldn't keep our hands away from each other. We thought we were too unimportant to be noticed.

"One day my aunt saw us together, and she told my parents. When I returned to the apartment and my waiting parents, my mother accused me of being a public spectacle. I burst out with the truth: I loved Lucia and someday we would be together and love each other forever. My father took off his belt and used the buckle end on me. It ripped through my blouse and lacerated my skin. When my parents told Lucia's family, they transferred her to another school. For two years, my family hardly spoke to me. Without a word, Mama set up a small table next to the dining table. There I was to eat alone when they had finished their meals. During that time, I shriveled in my soul. When I was eighteen, they arranged for me to marry a widower who owned a small Spanish restaurant. They had told him about me and Lucia, and said he should beat me whenever he thought my Lesbianism might show up again— which he did. After two months I escaped to a battered woman's shelter. The social worker helped me to find a house-sharing situation and a job. One of the girls in the house became my lover, and we decided to go to secretarial school at night. When we completed our courses and got better jobs, we took our own apartment. When I called Mama one day and told her I was happy with a gentle, caring woman, she screamed at me that I should have stayed married. It was better to appear respectable no matter how my husband treated me, rather than live as I live in 'mortal sin.' May my whole family drop dead in 'mortal pain.'"

BIFF: *"I'm not good enough to raise their kids"*

There has been little exploration into the realm of Gay people and their brothers and sisters, but it seems to me that when parents are gone, the brothers and sisters may carry on the sense of family. I envision a generation of siblings—Gay or straight—who open their doors and their hearts to each other. Biff, a twenty-six-year-old upwardly mobile executive, told me this story:

"My brother and sister-in-law were blasé about my being Gay. I was invited to all their parties to show their friends how tuned in they were to the contemporary world. But somehow I felt I was being used. As the congenial uncle of their six- and eight-year-old boys, I taught them chess, bestowed lavish gifts on them and took them to every 'in' kid happening in New York. I was also graciously permitted to give my dear brother and his wife the down payment on their condo, minus interest. Okay? I thought I had a family until one day the three of us discussed our wills. Since my brother and I share property, we decided to use the same lawyer. When the lawyer asked who would raise the kids in the event of their death, I said I would be honored.

"The two looked stricken. Then my sister-in-law said, 'Oh, no. Not you. I want my kids to have a normal life—not to be surrounded by fairies. My sister can take the boys and bring them up with her six kids. They would have cousins to play with and a normal upbringing.'

"I was shocked. If she had used 'normal' one more time, I would have let her have it. In my eyes, my love for my nephews was 'normal.' I have money for their comfort, well-being and a singular interest in their development. How could she prefer her dragged-out sister with six kids pulling on her to me? Sure, it's because I'm Gay and not good enough to raise their kids.

"Although their premature death together is remote, I know our breach was brought on by their underlying homophobia. Still, it spells out a message to me loud and clear that they consider me unfit. Of course, it hurts."

MAVIS: "Someone on my side"

Mavis is a chubby—well, fat—young Lesbian woman who still smolders over her mother's ridicule.

"My mother has asked me if I became Lesbian because she had always made fun of me. I told her, 'Probably.' She would try to shame me into losing weight by making fun of me in front of other people. For instance, when we were shopping in the underwear department, she would tell the saleswoman that I wore a forty-two-long bra size. When I once lost fifty pounds, she said no one would notice. When I got all A's in college, I called her. Do you know what she said? She said, 'That was lucky, Mavis.' *Lucky*? If one of my brothers who studies woodwork brings home a little whittled doll, she tells him he's a genius. I'm sick of her not-so-gentle hints about my weight. When I visited her last week, she shoved a pair of queen-size pantyhose at me, telling me they were on sale at Alexander's.

"Now I've come out to her and invited her to dinner to meet my lover, who is fat and forty. I love every delicious pound of her. We have so much fun together. My mother's curiosity about my life-style finally got the best of her, and she came over. When I told her the dessert was called 'Chocolate Orgasmic Pie' she threw down her napkin and left.

"She's really pissed that I have a great life with my lover and that together we enjoy music, theater and food. We just enjoy. Period. That's what galls my mother. She doesn't mind that I'm a Lesbian as much as she minds losing control over me. My lover doesn't let her get away with anything where I'm concerned. I now have not only a lover and a wonderful new life, but someone on my side for the first time. My mother, who's dainty and pretty, acts out her hostility toward me for not being her ideal. I have the feeling that if I were a sexy-looking beauty and she could shine in my light, she wouldn't care if I were a Lesbian."

BERNARD: "It's so much easier to be Gay and young today"

Bernard's memories and regrets are sadly real. But at least he has lived to see how times have changed and will hopefully continue to change so that closeness with a Gay family member will not be at all unusual. Bernard, a handsome and debonair Gay attorney in his early sixties, is a full partner in a well-known midtown law firm, which caters mostly to a theatrical practice.

"When my father emigrated from Russia during open pogrom season in the early 1900s, he planted himself on the Lower East Side as a tailor, and there he stayed for the rest of his life. He married my mother, who came from the same little hamlet, and they had four sons. My eldest brother died in the influenza epidemic of 1918. My mother, who had inherited some insurance money from her parents, decided to invest it in an uptown bar with her brother. Although my mother arrived in the United States one year before my father, she spoke mostly Yiddish all her life. After the contract for the bar was signed by my mother and uncle, my uncle confessed to my mother that their bar was frequented by 'fairies.' My mother's answer—'So vot, ve'll flit—ve'll call the extoiminator' —is legend in our family. She hadn't the remotest idea of what a 'fairy' was.

"For me, it was a Gay boy's dream. I tended bar from my mid to late teens. I met my lover there when I was twenty-two, and it seems as though we have been married forever: comfortable, caring, sharing. Isn't that what everyone wants?

"When I came out to my parents, they were hysterical for two years. But, strangely enough, they stopped the attacks and never mentioned it again. My 'friend' or 'buddy,' as my parents decided to call him, was sometimes—sometimes not—included in family functions. We were not seen as a couple by them. I suppose they figure that if they didn't look at the Gay issue, it would go away. I don't believe that they ever addressed him directly. It was always, 'Ask your friend if he wants more meat. Ask "him" if he would pass the salt.'

"When my parents died, we became involved with my brothers and their families, who would invite us for holidays and other family doings. But it's never occurred to us that they would ever consider coming to *our* apartment with their children. Now, of course, the pattern is set, and we continue as always with the same unspoken relationship. We are still the perennial guests who do not reciprocate; we are sure that they would not come.

"I have regrets. I regret not having the opportunity to host the family. I grew up in an atmosphere of hospitality and warmth. Yet being host to my brothers and parents was something I could never have done in those years. My family has never even seen where I live—and I live well. We entertain a lot. When we were invited together, we felt like *auslanders*; when I was invited separately, I felt like an isolate. Today it's different. I see many Gay youngsters and their lovers making holiday dinners, parties, wedding showers, bachelor dinner for their families. It's easier today."

ROGER: "It's not a doorknob"

Roger's story is another classic story of rejection. Roger, a fifty-five-year-old accountant in business for himself says:

"Our high school principal was rigid in his belief that boys and girls should be separate in their social activities. So starched was his attitude that when we gave school dances, he insisted that boys dance with boys and girls dance with girls. This was so there would be no 'problems.'

"When I was fourteen, I knew I was Gay. I can't tell you how divine these dances were. But I'm off the track. You wanted to know how my family reacted to me. Well, I was eighteen and leading my lover up the stairs by the you-know-what while he protested that it was not a door-knob. Suddenly in burst my folks. Being old-fashioned people, they were apoplectic, to say the least. To this day they refer to me bitterly as the 'gayzy.' There is always a bitter exchange when I visit. But they take my financial help."

MINNA: "I was endowed with good fortune"

Minna's story—she is a thirty-year-old Lesbian—has a happy ending. I love it. Minna says:

"I was married for ten years but had always pushed my real self away. Although I had been attracted to other women, I never acted out and had never been in love. From the standpoint of my parents, I was endowed with good fortune. I had a hand-some, hardworking husband, an adorable child of five and a stately Georgian home in the not-too-deep South. I also had my own small but thriving business—a tennis shop where I sold apparel and equipment. I played the part of the devoted wife but deep inside I carried with me the sense of dishonesty.

"Last year I met Vivian. She just walked into the shop. We talked, looked at each other and were instantly attracted. My conventional world receded. Vivian practically bought out the shop, including an expensive graphite racquet. From that day on, we played tennis, always rallying, never wanting to compete against each other.

Every stroke of the ball—it was a sexual thing really—was a protest against the rules we had been living by. We knew we had to be together. When I told my husband, he took it gallantly. We discussed divorce. He insisted on meeting Vivian. It was like an audition because he wanted to know the kind of person who would soon be part of his child's environment. She got the part. They even shook hands. He arranged to see our child on the weekends and vacations of his choice. Vivian was single, so there were no complications on her side. We moved to a nearby town and together opened a sporting goods shop.

"My parents? My mom and dad were both shocked at first naturally. But they were resilient and forward-thinking people. They jumped in with both feet to learn what they could about being Gay. They sent for an armful of books from a Washington Gay affirmative organization which would take care of their reading about alternative sexuality for at least a year. They joined a church support group. They asked Vivian, me and our new Lesbian friends how, what, who, why, when? Finally they were satisfied. Whatever they went through to understand what had happened to the straight little girl they once thought they knew, they went through privately. They were their own self-help group. They said they trusted my ex-husband, Vivian and me to give their grandchild the love and support she will need in the years ahead."

MAE: "I admitted to myself that I, too, was Gay"

Mae was orphaned at seventeen when both parents were killed in an automobile accident. She went to live with her aunt and the woman her aunt had lived with, closeted, for thirty years.

"My aunt's friends were non-Gay. The two women blended harmoniously into small-town life, totally accepted.

"When I was nineteen and had gone off to college, I admitted to myself that I, too, was Gay. But I was not about to go underground with it. I became active in the college Gay student club. When I came home to my aunt for the holidays, she told me that she was dismayed. That I would 'upset the applecart.' I realized that she was typical of her generation. I cannot—will not—live as they have. So I moved out. I am sad about it. They were good to me."

•   •   •

These children are self-identified as Gay. For some, coming out meant expulsion from their families either physically and/or emotionally. Many were hurt and bitter about the schism that resulted. But, fortunately, there were those Gay children who were gratified to have blazed a new trail right into their parents center. They found acceptance and recognition: years of pent-up feelings burst forth and masks were off as parents and children really communicated at last. I hope that the time is drawing near when more and more Gay children will be so received. And I believe that the time will come sooner as more and more experts believe that parents should accept their Gay children without feelings of shame and disgrace.

What Some Experts Say

Whatever advantages may have arisen, in the
past, out of the existence of a specially
favored and highly privileged aristocracy, it
is clear to me that today no argument can
stand that supports unequal opportunity or any
intrinsic disqualification for sharing
in the whole of life.

—Margaret Mead, *Blackberry Winter*

What does a parent stand to gain by acceptance of a Gay child? What does a parent stand to lose by denial of a Gay child? I put these questions to various and sundry professionals: social workers, educators, psychiatrists, psychologists and members of the clergy. Most accused me of asking loaded questions. To this charge I unabashedly admit guilt. I excuse myself, however, because there is no shortage of biased thinking about homosexuality. There *is* a shortage of positive thinking.

Alma H. Bond, Ph.D., psychoanalyst, New York City:

"I believe a parent has everything to gain by the acceptance of a child's homosexuality. Children should be loved unconditionally, and accepted for what they are. Parents who require a child to fill a certain preconceived mold before loving the child are not loving parents at all, and will lose their children sooner or later, whatever the child's sexual orientation. Secondly, I believe that those who cannot accept homosexuality in a child are not in touch with their own instinctual life. All of us have known homosexual impulses to some degree, at some time or other, for all children experience a love of both parents which knows no sexual boundaries. Many people fear that they will act out these wishes, and therefore repress all knowledge of them. Homosexuality in their children threatens those homophobic parents who are terrified of acknowledging their own unconscious instinctual wishes."

The Reverend Channing E. Phillips, Riverside Church, New York City:

"By acceptance, the parent gains a continuing relationship with the child and is in a better position to assist the child in coping with his identity. In denial, the parent runs the danger of losing the child and risks adversely affecting the development of the child: the child is then torn between his own feelings and what he thinks the world needs to perceive."

Rabbi Balfour Brickner, Stephen Wise Free Synagogue, New York City:

"In acceptance, you stand to gain your child. In denial, you stand to lose your child. It's simple. Perhaps a parent gets a sense of justification through vindictiveness if he or she wants to self-justify. It could be that the parent who is critically condemning of homosexuality gains self-justification consistent with his or her own bias. It is so much easier and more acceptable to be homosexual today than in the past—even in the smaller towns."

Rabbi Harvey Tattelbaum, Temple Shaaray Tefila, New York City:

"I would tell a parent not to lose the love of a child and the relationship with him or her; not to look for explanations, not to feel guilty, and to always relate to the child. Denial of a child would be wrong. I would bring the parent to the level of coping with the child and the situation. I am not guided by ancient traditions on this matter, which come down very heavily on homosexuality. One must transcend the sense of condemnation and restrictiveness and not forget the human being, who, very often, is in pain."

Dr. F. Forrester Church, minister, All Souls Unitarian Church, New York City:

"My usual response is to encourage parents to embrace children as they are; the act of reconciliation is in and of itself a redemptive and healing act. I see nothing to be gained by denial."

Jay Greene, Ed.D., retired member and chairman of the New York City Board of Examiners for the Board of Education:

"A child who is Gay is going to have a difficult life and a difficult time in making a living. Where else should a child turn for love, guidance and understanding, if not to a parent. It is unthinkable to lose the love of a child because of a lack of understanding."

Miriam Lahey, Ph.D., gerontologist, New York City:

"A rejecting parent has everything to lose. First, they lose the relationship. It has nothing to do with the child, but has everything to do with themselves in that closing themselves off to the reality of a situation is like choosing death. What a parent has to gain, in acceptance, is exactly the opposite—a relationship with their child as other; the otherness gives the relationship an added dimension."

Maralyn Lowenheim, M.S.W., psychiatric social worker, Brooklyn, New York:

"Accepting the Gay child means giving up the hope and fantasy that the child will change his/her sexual preference. It means accepting the child for who he/she is, without the expectation that the child must conform to the parents' needs and wishes in order to be part of the family. Giving up the fantasy frees the parent to acknowledge and affirm the child to respect him/her. By not accepting the Gay child, the parent can anticipate the ultimate loss of the child as an integral member of the family. Nonacceptance places a great strain on the relationship, indicating to the child that parental love is contingent upon conforming behavior, rather than being unconditional and without proviso, obligations and ultimatums."

Dr. Leo Schneller, psychiatrist, New York State:

Dr. Schneller limited his answer to parental relationships with adult children. He felt that if a parent is genuinely accepting, he had much to gain. Acceptance must be accompanied by mutual respect and regard, which, of course, is beneficial to both parents and offspring. The rejecting parent stands to lose the comfort and satisfaction of a lifelong relationship.

Here is another "expert" opinion:

A group in New York City claims the ability to engender change from homosexuality to heterosexuality. The parents in this group assert that their Gay sons have triumphed over what they believe to be perversity rather than diversity. They believe that a major cause of homosexuality is excessive mother love, which results in a basic contempt for all women. Because Mom was such an easy conquest, they believe, all women are easy conquests. Thus: no quarry, no hunt. The male instinct to conquer is thwarted.

These parents of Gay sons told me how this "cure" is effected. A triumvirate of male members converse in depth with the would-be converts—supposedly finding the cause of their homosexuality. The man being "treated" admits his contempt for women (the name of the game is really misogyny), then this Gay person is on the road to recovery from his "illness."

The parents were a veritable Greek chorus rejoicing over their rehabilitated sons. But their rhetoric sounded hollow. Was it possible that not one son had experienced failure? In effect what they said could be summarized thus: "We were crushed. We decided to use any means whatsoever to rehabilitate him. We were behind him—pushing. Our son is now married to a lovely girl. They have a child (or two). Our son has returned from the dead."

The parents were perfectly attuned in their unison. Their sons had married "lovely" girls. All seemed to be new grandparents. I had the impression that they had all been dunked in a kind of Lourdes of heterosexuality. If there was so much success, why hasn't the medical and mental health community not acknowledged this group?

I wondered also about the future of their brides if and when the Gay person inside of these men reasserts himself. How long can the "ex-Gay" men suppress their feelings?

My problem with this ideology is that there has been no substantiated explanation as to why erotic orientation develops. Furthermore, there is no empirical proof of permanent change.

Here's what some authorities say about change:

- Dr. C. A. Tripp in *The Homosexual Matrix* says that no change from Gay to non-Gay has been validated.

- Dr. William Pomeroy offered to administer the Kinsey Research battery to a homosexual a therapist might send and thus perhaps validate a case of turncoat homosexuality. (There was only one taker.)

- Dr. George Weinberg in *Society and the Healthy Homosexual* notes that Dr. Irving Bieber's study which measured change was invalid because he chose psychiatrically disturbed patients in treatment as his sample.

- Dr. Ralph Blair wrote in *Ex-Gay* that " . . . there is still no documented empirical verification of any permanent change from homosexual orientation to heterosexual orientation through the 'Ex-Gay' processes." Dr. Blair writes that there is plenty of evidence of diagnostic error, self-deception and other manifestations that counter claims of "Ex-Gays."

- Susan Frankel, MSW, a former director at the New York Institute of Human Identity, finds that although certain Gay and Lesbian clients do come out as Gay and Lesbian and then attempt reversal, these changes do not appear to affect a deep internal sense of themselves. These people are beset by severe narcissistic identity problems.

Interestingly, the group of which I speak was formed in 1973, just about the time that the American Psychiatric Association declared that homosexuality is not a mental disorder, per se. Apparently this pronouncement and the opinions of some of the experts quoted here did not make homosexuality all right for many Gay people and their parents. Of course, one should be free to make the switch if the switch is possible.

But I feel that these parents have imposed *their* beliefs upon their adult Gay sons. Such a "metamorphosis" (which I doubt is possible) is contrary to their children's basic nature.

WARNING: Parents should question the group that promises "miraculous" changes in their children's fundamental sexuality. Such promises rarely bring fulfillment. They are like candy offered to the hungry: such candy provides no nutritional value. Rather it would behoove parents to face up to the reality that if a child is Gay, it is "natural" for him or her to be Gay. And if their son or daughter is encouraged to suppress homosexual tendencies for the sake of conformity, severe problems may later arise. It would be more beneficial to concentrate on achieving and maintaining a comfortable relationship with a Gay child.

The Workshops for Families of Gay People

Risk! Risk anything! Care no more for the
opinion of others, for those voices. Do
the hardest thing on earth for you.
Act for yourself.

—Katherine Mansfield, *The Journal of Katherine Mansfield*

When I finally completed my master's in social work and passed the state certification examination, I was set to look for a job in the mental health field. Still thinking I might find an organization that sponsored a professionally led group for the families of Gay people, I continued to search for such a group: one that would meet weekly and be small enough so that participants could comfortably exchange ideas. In the sprawling New York megalopolis where I live, I could not find such a group. I would have to initiate a group myself.

Why not? To date, such a bewildering assortment of human dilemmas was being dealt with in groups led by experienced professionals. When I was a young woman, I never dreamed that so many people would bare their souls about adultery, intermarriage, divorce, open marriage, contraceptive methods, abortions, and unrestricted sexuality. You name the problem: the group to help solve it was there. Except for one ubiquitous human dilemma: the homosexuality of a son, daughter or other family member.

Why not? Where was this group? Were the professionals too beset by their own homophobia to reach out to the families of Gay people? I have no pat answer. And the reason was—and is—beyond the scope of my inquiry. What *was* within the scope of my inquiry was to find the means for these families to gather together so that they, too, might have the comfort of unburdening themselves and putting forth their questions.

I had already counseled parents of Gay children individually and in small groups, but because I continued to believe this was a community and social work concern, I looked for an *organization* that would sponsor workshops.

I was not disappointed. I found the YWCA.* Directors Chris Filner, of the New York City Y, and Sandra Jenkins, of the White Plains, New York Y, decided to act upon the purpose of the Young Woman's Christian Association (now celebrating its 125th birthday): "to open lives to new understanding and deeper relationships and that together they may join in the struggle for peace and justice, freedom and dignity for all people."

For the fall of 1984, the 92nd Street Y had also scheduled a workshop for the families of Gay people— a first for this prestigious Jewish organization. Would it not be gratifying to see such workshops spring up in other community organizations all over the country!

The following chapter outlines what we do in the workshops. Although I do not rigidly limit myself to the outline, I do try to keep us on track as much as possible. In the first session, I attempt to set our sights with the following declaration: "We are not here to examine the how and the why our children turned out

*YWCA Women's Center Directors.

to be Gay. The medical community has not yet come up with definitive answers to this question. Explanations are still speculative. If it is so important to you to attach blame or find a reason, perhaps one day scientists will come up with an amniocentesis test to determine sexual orientation. But seriously, does it really matter now to you as the parent or relative of a Gay person? Let us just start from where we are now."

WORKSHOPS FOR
FAMILIES OF GAY PEOPLE

Six Sessions:

A positive approach designed to help you share and sort out feelings, shorten emotional distance, help reintegrate the loved Gay person into the family more comfortably and learn from and communicate with other relatives of Gay people. The group is structured and informative. Articles will be distributed and readings suggested.

Week I: Who are we? Self-disclosure.

Week II: Perceptions and misperceptions about homosexuality. Reactions and attitudes toward our Gay children.

Week III: Historical overview. Guest speaker. What was it like for our Gay children?

Week IV: Getting philosophical. Optional religious discussion.

Week V: We invite the children. Open the lines of communication.

Week VI: We summarize present feelings. What are changes wrought by workshop? Discussion. Wine and cheese party.

Has dealing with the fact of a Gay son or daughter strengthened your ability to deal with other challenging life situations?*

A TYPICAL SAMPLE COMPOSITE WORKSHOP
(Twelve to Nineteen Members)

We sit in a large room around an oblong table rather than in the traditional circle of dangling hands and feet. We sprawl comfortably, and sip soft drinks and coffee. We unwind, work to establish trust, hear and see each other, and sense each other's eagerness to talk about this subject which has so long lay dormant within us or had been such a bone of contention in our lives.

The assumption is that the presence of participants at these workshops indicates that they are unwilling to lose their Gay adult children without making some effort to keep the lines of communication open. They are attempting to do this by coming to the workshop to learn how to better understand their children.

Week I: Introduction

Before I circle the room, inviting introductions and self-disclosure, I begin with myself. I define my situa-

*Although I try to keep to the above outline, the group sometimes prefers to approach their problems differently and I defer to their lead.

tion as the parent of a Gay son, briefly sketch my background and tell about my search for a group such as this, where I could have talked to others in the same situation, under the umbrella of a respected community organization. I do not promise the proverbial rose garden, but I state our goal: to step forward in our relationships with our Gay children.

I acknowledge the problems we have with this goal, among them the dichotomy between the position taken by the American Psychiatric Association that homosexuality is not a mental disturbance and the influence of the people who say it is—those whose thinking is far from Socratic and who would deny our children their human rights.

I acknowledge that bigots who would hammer their intolerant views into so many of us have been tragically successful and that we must strive to deprogram ourselves of such bigotry and head in the direction of love for and understanding of our Gay children.

I admit that the readings I suggest and the printed matter that I distribute are Gay affirmative. We have been inundated with negative information about Gay people far too long and cannot reconcile this negativity with the Gay child we know and love. I acknowledge that even though my concern is family and we are not gathered for the purpose of examining Gay rights issues, we must nevertheless disabuse ourselves of some of the feelings engendered by the words of hatred and illogic spoken by those who are purely and simply homophobic. (I explain that this word *homophobic* was coined in 1967 by Dr. George Weinberg and means "irrational revulsion of homosexuality.")

I then come down from my soapbox and give the group members a chance to speak up. And speak up they do. They plunge right in, eager to air their feelings. It is apparent that most of them have bottled up these feelings for a long time. They have been closeted about their adult children's sexuality, unable to breathe easily, and that secrecy is becoming a burden that taps their psychic energy.

They are quite a mix—retired people, housewives, businessmen and women, social workers, teachers, an engineer, an electrician, a surgeon, a lawyer, a detective. These dissimilar individuals from dissimilar background share a common bond: they are all parents of Gay children. (Almost all: we do have one sister of a Gay brother.) I distribute booklets from the National Gay Task Force—"Answers to a Parent's Questions about Homosexuality" and "Twenty Questions about Homosexuality"—and catalogs from such Gay bookstores as Lambda Rising (Washington, D.C.), A Different Light (New York City,) the Oscar Wilde Memorial Bookshop (New York City), and the library catalog of the National Federation of Parents and Friends of Gays (Washington, D.C.). I also give out a list of terms we'll be using.

DEFINITION OF TERMS

Androgynous (from the Greek *andre* "man" and *gyne* "woman"): having both masculine and feminine traits.

Bi-Sexual: one who has sexual and emotional responses to both sexes.

Coming Out: adopted by Lesbians and Gay men to describe the process of becoming aware of and expressing one's identity. "Coming out of the closet" is a metaphor for telling people about one's Lesbian or Gay identity.

Dyke: applied to Lesbians, usually negatively, to

stereotype them as "masculine," much as *fairy* has been used to stereotype "feminine" men. Recently some Lesbians have begun to use the word as a term of pride to mean a strong and independent woman.

Faggot (from a Latin word meaning "a bundle of sticks"): applied to Gays during the Inquisition when they were burned along with "witches." ("Only a faggot could produce a flame foul enough to burn a witch.")

Gay: one of the few terms applied to homosexuals that has been adopted by them as a sign of pride. While Gay is sometimes used to refer to both men and women, it generally refers to men; Lesbians usually prefer to be called Lesbians.

Heterosexism: a belief in the superiority of heterosexuality; policies and practices that serve to elevate heterosexuality and subordinate homosexuality.

Heterosexual: one who has sexual and affectional responses predominantly to the opposite sex. (It is interesting to note that there are no negative or derogatory terms for a heterosexual.)

Homophobia: a fear and hatred of Gay men and Lesbians.

Homosexual: a clinical term for people whose sexual/affectional preference is for members of the same sex.

In the Closet: Lesbians or Gay men who feel unable to tell others that they are Lesbian or Gay. A person may, for example, be "in the closet" on their job or with their family in order to avoid discrimination or rejection.

Lesbian (from the Greek isle of Lesbos, where the Lesbian poet Sappho had a school in 400 B.C.): one of the oldest and most positive terms for Gay women.

Sexuality: the psychic energy that finds physical and emotional expression in the desire for contact, warmth, tenderness and love.

Sexual Orientation: a natural and inborn personal characteristic that governs one's sexuality.

Sexual Preference: the instinctive choice of partners according to gender... providing evidence of an individual's sexual orientation.

Straight: used by both heterosexuals and Lesbians and Gay men to refer to heterosexuals.

Transsexual: a person who feels he/she really belongs to the opposite sex. For example, a man may feel he is really a female in all ways but is trapped in a male body. This is not at all the same as being Gay.

Transvestite: a man who gets erotic pleasure from dressing in women's clothes. This is also not at all the same as being Gay.

• • •

After I finish my introduction and the parents have scanned the material, they look up expectantly. I wait for them to introduce themselves. Brick, a ruddy-faced man wearing a sports jacket over a bright red sweater, proves to be the catalyst for the group. He voices thoughts and asks questions that are representative of what is going on inside most of the group members.

"I would rather be anywhere else but here—at a workshop like this, but I need to be here. Five years ago my younger daughter, Amy, told me she was Gay, and I threw her out of the house—practically bodily. Now we have an armed truce, but I cringe when my golf buddies ask why isn't a pretty girl like Amy married? Boy, do they have a nice date for her—their own sons or nephews, of course."

The flow of talk starts. Other parents speak up. No formality. No taking of turns. Simply spontaneous feelings coming out. The desire to be known, to be heard about concerns pressing to all of them is up-front. They are adults and, as adults, make their own decisions about how they want to conduct the discussions. I step in to keep us on course so that we will stay within the scheduled issues if the talk threatens to wander too far afield. But within the framework of the format, there is as much play as they want.

Wilma, slim, fashionably dressed and meticulously groomed, says that she has two children—a boy and a girl—by her first marriage, which ended in divorce. The boy, nineteen-year-old Teddy, had come out to her several months before. Recently married and accompanied by her obviously tense new husband, Wilma reports:

> "Not only am I contending with a new marriage, a new community and a new life, but I now face the dilemma of trying to deal with a new son. It's putting a terrible strain on our marriage. My husband is uncomfortable with my son now, and I feel overwhelmed. I refuse to apologize to people about my son, yet I don't know him now. I wonder if I ever did."

James, a gangly man who introduces himself as a tax attorney, a recent widower and father of a Gay son *and* daughter, asks us if we think he is a snob because he admires his son Lucas's success as an attorney and wonders if his outstanding professional success contributes to his unhesitating acceptance of homosexuality. On the other hand, his daughter Barbara, also Gay, is a nonachiever in her father's eyes. James guiltily admits that he finds her Lesbianism unpalatable.

Shelly, a dark-haired, olive-skinned divorced woman who emigrated from Cuba twelve years ago, tells our incredulous group how she has been a battered wife and tried to raise her three children as best she could. Three years ago, they came out to her as Gay: one by one, year after year:

> "I am with them now, all the way. But I feel over my head and without direction in how I can best deal with them. I have been longing to interact with other parents of Gay children. I lost a child five years ago in a drowning accident. These three— my two teenage daughters, Ella and Carmen, and my twenty-one-year-old son Jose are all I have left. I'd rather have them Gay than not have them at all."

An elderly woman who would become the group's conscience takes her turn:

> "My name is Fern. I'm a seventy-eight-year-old widow and I feel riddled with guilt about the way I treated my Gay son, Louis, who is now forty. I mistreated him. Louis came out to me twenty years ago when it was not all right with the medical—or any other—community. Now I seethe with anger about the way most people treat Gays. The jokes. The contempt. The cruelties. I want to make it up to Louis, but it's late in the day for that. I came here because I need to talk about regret."

Mr. and Mrs. A. are a white-haired, dour-faced, retired couple in the process of moving to Florida. Mrs. A., her voice soft and hesitant, speaks for both:

> "Our daughter, Marie, is Gay. She is thirty-three and living in the fast lane in Hollywood as an executive with a major film studio. When Marie was little, she had a rheumatic heart and is much too delicate to live the way she does with her—

uh—inamorata. We want Marie to come to Florida with us. We could take care of her, and she would have the peace and quiet her health demands. Of course, she doesn't agree with us that she is not strong, but we know she's not strong. We need her and she needs us. That...woman is a bad influence on her."

While Mrs. A. talks, her husband nods in agreement. Then Mr. B., a tall, Viking-type man, leans forward:

"My name is Mr. B., and this is my wife. We are Swedish, and we both come from reserved, conservative families. It's hard for us to be so frank about our feelings. We're like our parents were— couples who sat around sighing whenever a crisis arose. They were rather like the people in *Cries and Whispers*. When Nils, our son who is nineteen, told us he was...ah, uh...Gay...last month, there was a terrible donnybrook in our usually peaceful family. My wife didn't react as badly as I did. Nils moved out and now stays with a brother-in-law I dislike. I love Nils. I don't want to lose him, but I can't reach him. He won't talk to me on the telephone. I told him when he first came out that I hate what he is. But now I know that I want to understand him. My feelings about homosexuality will never change. But I must learn more about my son. *Just my son*. Not his...friends. I tell you this so that you will respect how I feel and not try to change my unsympathetic feelings."

In this instance, Mr. B. does the talking for the couple and Mrs. B. listens, nodding in agreement with what her husband says. I speak up now.

"That's all right. Perhaps after you have learned to understand more about Nils, you'll understand more about other people's children. I don't intend to exert any pressure in this group. You feel as you feel, and if you choose to bend a bit—or not—it's your own choice. You're not going to be Indian-wrestled to the ground until you say, 'Uncle! Gay is great!' You will move forward at your own pace. At least I hope you will. But, as I said earlier, you'll be exposed to positive rather than negative attitudes. Take what you will from it."

An attractive blond woman who has been looking intently at the speakers now raises her hand. Before she speaks, I remind the group: "You're not in class. This is a *workshop*. I have the confidence that you will all allow each other spontaneous input without having to be 'called upon' formally when you have something to say."

The woman, who then introduces herself as Mrs. C. and her husband as Mr. C., tells us that he is a New York City detective. Mr. C., smiling wryly, speaks:

"I've hauled in more male prostitutes than I can ever track. In my head I know there are high-caliber Gays, but I keep seeing them all as the ones I've arrested. Now, Mike, my son, tells me he's one of them. I can't hack it. Especially when a high-pitched voice calls him on the phone and tells me his name is Bruce."

This bothers Mrs. C., too: some of her son's friends are "too noticeable."

A beautiful red-haired woman sits quietly huddled in a sable coat. Finally one of the participants asks her about herself. She looks at us, reddening, takes a deep breath and in a staccato voice, defines her problem:

"My name is Gerry. I probably don't belong here. You people *only* have Gay children. That's an easy one. My son has had the surgery that changes one's sex. He is no longer my son. This...person now tells me that 'she' is my daughter. But 'she' is not my daughter. I didn't give birth to a daughter. I gave birth to a boy. A son. This...person... tells me that he felt as a boy that he was in the wrong body. He belonged in a female body. I never saw the slightest hint of a wrong body. I never knew anything was wrong at all."

"I still don't believe this, even though it happened one year ago. I have no idea where to go to talk about it. Not that I'm able to even think about it in detail. So I'm here. I saw the Y catalog and I'm here."

We are stunned. The group is quiet for a while. Then I break the silence:

"Gerry, as long as you've already taken this step to do something about getting yourself some help— some relief, about what must have been tremendously shocking for you, it might behoove you to stay with us for a while. See how some of us deal with diversity. You might start with a process of desensitization for yourself by talking about your son's transformation."

Gerry shrugs: "What can I lose now?"

I think about her words that we *only* have Gay children. How our problems pale next to hers. Isn't there a saying about feeling sorry that you have no shoes until you meet a man who has no feet?

Mr. and Mrs. D., the youngest parents in the group, have four children. Their oldest, eighteen-year-old Elinor, has told them that she is Gay and has asked that she have the freedom of the house to entertain her Gay friends. After all, she reasons, her sixteen-year-old brother has the freedom at home to invite his non-Gay friends. Mrs. D., angry and challenged, feels this would be a bad influence on the younger children. Mr. D., less intense, tells us when he inquired about the whereabouts of our meeting room, he mumbled from behind his hand to the receptionist on the ground floor that he was looking for "that group." The receptionist, a substitute that night, hesitated, but then, despite Mr. D.'s look of embarrassment, nodded and spoke shrilly: "Oh, are you looking for the Family Workshop? It's on the ninth floor." Mr. D. tells us that he had turned beet-red and backed into the elevator, thankful that he was the tallest so he could avoid looking anyone in the eye by staring out over the heads of his fellow passengers. "But actually," says Mr. D. philosophically, "no one paid any attention to me. I'll probably get used to all this in time."

Mr. and Mrs. E., both accountants dressed in navy blue three-piece suits, glance at each other. Mr. E. says he can cope with their son Harry's homosexuality, but not with Harry's brutish and hostile lover. Since Harry has been seeing this lover, he has noticed that his son often has a black eye. I comment that the purpose of this workshop was to discuss and learn more about homosexuality so as to better understand our Gay children. However, we are not going to deal with destructive or violent Gay relationships, which I compare to the pathology of the battered wife situation. I suggest that this couple probe the subject of homosexuality along with us, but urge their son to see a qualified therapist to discover why he seeks and tolerates violence in a relationship (or to take boxing lessons!).

Mr. and Mrs. G. are a frail, elderly couple at a loss as to how to deal with their daughter, Jane—a physicist and mother of three children—who left her husband of ten years to move in with the woman next door. The G.'s, pillars of their community and doting grandparents, want to keep the family intact. They love their son-in-law and think that Jane's life, with its palatial home, social standing and frequent trips to Europe, was ideal. Mrs. G., holding hands with her husband throughout the evening, says wistfully,

> "Jane is my only daughter. We were so close. Or at least I thought we were. How could she do this to her wonderful husband, to her children and to us? All these years was she another person rather than who I thought she was?"

No one can answer this question.

Interestingly, there are several widows in the group whose Gay sons came out to them after the loss of their fathers. Each woman—and I identified with them—expresses the usual reactions: a sense of helplessness, a fear of family and friends finding out, and difficulty in relating to their Gay children as comfortably as they had prior to disclosure. One woman is self-employed, another is a bank official and the others are working at part-time jobs, retired or about to retire. Very much in step with the eighties, they are verbal, capable women, but, as I have seen frequently, these parents are frustrated and perplexed when it comes to coping with the reality of a Gay child.

I wonder why so many Gay children came out to widowed mothers. Are they counting on the ever-ready wells of maternalism to gush forth no matter what? Do they feel the coast is clear now that they do not have to face a probable apoplectic paternal reaction—as one mother suggests? I recall reading about research that shows mothers of Gay sons to be more accepting than fathers. Perhaps, I think, most mothers and Gay sons share a common bond—they both love men.

Mr. and Mrs. H.—he has his own insurance company, she is a high school English teacher—conclude the first session by telling us about their beautiful daughter, Gilda, a doctoral candidate at a local university. Gilda, financially dependent upon her parents, still lives at home with them while finishing her studies. When she told them she was Gay and in love with a student, they were catapulted into a state of shock. Mr. H. says, "We cannot reconcile her being Gay with our religious beliefs as practicing Catholics."

I say that we are running out of time and rather than begin a discussion of the church's views toward Gays, I will bring material on religion and homosexuality next week.

There we have it. Middle-aged, middle-class America. Good people. Caring people. Off to a start. They have spoken about their Gay children to each other.

We run overtime. There is an insistent knocking at the door. The drama group, who follows us in the use of the meeting room, is more than impatient. When I open the door, they glare. But I am helpless. The parents, oblivious to the irritated Thespians, fall upon each other in nonstop conversation. Ears! They have found ears at last! It will be a struggle each week to gently urge them toward the door to let the next group in. I hear my workshop parents arranging to meet at nearby coffee shops. What is the song, "Now that I've found you, I'll never let you go"? They wave good night.

After I get home, I make an entry in my Workshop Notebook:

...mostly a cross section of thinking New York area people who are the parents of one or more Gay children...people with family pride...people who

142

need to fathom the depths of a controversial subject on their own... people who are resisting social attitudes that would have them turn against their Gay children... people in the throes of family dynamics that might take place in any family, whether or not the children are Gay.

Week II: Perceptions and Feelings

The parents are caught up in animated conversation as they settle themselves in preparation for our second meeting. They have apparently established a rapprochement, seeing each other as welcome sounding boards and comrades in arms.

I open with a paraphrased quotation from the widely read psychologist George Weinberg, Ph.D., author of *Society and the Healthy Homosexual*, who writes that most of us as parents find it unnatural to shun our Gay children and that John Money, Ph.D., professor of medical psychology and pediatrics at Johns Hopkins Hospital says that we cannot account for the cause of homosexuality. I remind the group that we parents are not a trifling minority but over seventy million strong: that the twenty million Gay people in this country have millions of parents, siblings and grandparents. If only numerically, we are a potential force for family support systems for these Gay people. I distribute copies of a booklet,"Can We Understand?" a guide for parents prepared by the volunteer group, Parents of Gays and Lesbians, from New York City. The parents are reading it intently, noting the sensitive issues mentioned with which we all identify. I pass copies of a list of church organizations to show how the Gay rights movement is slowly changing the views of some churches:

American Baptists Concerned
198 Santa Clara Avenue
Oakland, CA 94610

Disciples of Christ
Rev. Robert Glover
Task Force on Human Sexuality
Post Office Box 1986
222 South Downey Avenue
Indianapolis, IN 46206

Brethren-Mennonite Gay Caucus
Martin Rock
Box 582
Lancaster, PA 17604

Friends Committee for
Gay Concerns
Box 222
Sumneytown, PA 18084

Kindred
(Seventh-Day Adventists)
Box 1233-A
Los Angeles, CA 90028

Integrity
(Protestant Episcopal)
Mr. John Lawrence
10 Mercier Avenue
Dorchester, MA 02124

Lutherans Concerned
(LCA, ALC, MO, SYNOD)
Mr. Diane Fraser/
Mr. Howard Erickson
Box 19114A
Los Angeles, CA 90019

Moravians Concerned
Rev. James A. Kennedy
632 North 4th Street
Philadelphia, PA 19123

Presbyterians for
Gay Concerns
Mr. Chris Glaser
Post Office Box 46412
Los Angeles, CA 90046

Unitarian Office for
Gay Concerns
Mr. Robert Wheatley
Unitarian Universalist Assoc.
25 Beacon Street
Boston, MA 02108

United Church of Christ
Dr. William R. Johnson
c/o Maranatha at
Riverside Church
490 Riverside Drive
New York, NY 10027

United Methodists for
Gay Concerns
Rev. Michael Collins
Post Office Box 775
New York, NY 10011

Universal Fellowship of
Metropolitan Community
Churches
5300 Santa Monica Blvd. No. 304
Los Angeles, CA 90029

Evangelicals Concerned
Dr. Ralph Blair
30 East 60th Street, Rm. 708
New York, NY 10022

Affirmation (Gay Mormon
Underground)
Post Office Box 9638
Denver, CO 80209

At this point the participants begin to question their earlier concepts.

Did our children choose this? Can we help them to change? Mother did it! Father did it! We both did it. Why? Why? Why my child? Why us? But what is it? Gay men swish, but my son doesn't. He was captain of the football team in high school. Plays murderous ice hockey. Lesbian women are rough, tough bull dykes, but my daughter isn't. She is a symbol of femininity. Why, it takes her hours to glue her individual lashes on.

Then, of course, there are those parents who talked about "sissy" sons and "Amazon" daughters. Descriptions follow of Gay children who fall somewhere in between. It is becoming clearer to the parents that Gay children could be a blend of incongruities just like the rest of us. Indeed, stereotypical categories might just be a fiction.

The parents look askance at each other. *"What have we been conned into believing?"* their expressions seem to ask. Doubts give way before the onslaught of each other's verbal pictures of their children.

We tackle one of the most insistent questions: *Why?*

I inform the group about a study by the Kinsey Institute which found a deep-seated predisposition to homosexuality. I pass out the article about the study which had been printed several years ago in *The New York Times*. Softly Wilma reads the passages aloud.

"Dr. Lawrence Hatterer, a New York psychiatrist who has studied the life histories of many homosexuals, said *he agreed with the Kinsey findings that sexual orientation was the result of a combination of many factors ... 'No particular phenomenon or family life can be singled out* [italics mine] on the basis of our findings, as especially consequential for either homosexual or heterosexual development,' the researchers state.

"What we seem to have identified is a pattern of feelings and reactions within the child that cannot be traced back to a single social or psychological root; indeed, homosexuality may arise from a biological precursor that parents cannot control."

Even though every member of the group appears to absorb the information, I find myself stressing again and again throughout the run of the workshop that *there is no known proven reason why we are sexually oriented as we are.* We leaf through the material from the Gay Task Force, and I read aloud:

"Gay and non-Gay children often grow up together in the same home ... homosexual feelings—affectional, emotional or erotic attraction to persons of one's own gender—are not a matter of choice. Neither are heterosexual feelings."

We flip the pages of the "Parents of Gays" booklet, stopping to read a paragraph:

"Homosexuality is not unnatural, since it exists in nature. It is just as natural for one person to be heterosexual as it is for another to be homosexual. We don't know why people are homosexual, but we know that there always were, are, and will be homosexuals."

Wilma brings her fist down on the table. She demands of no one in particular, "Why would anyone want to *choose* so difficult a path? I must believe that this is simply a condition of being."

Mr. B., who looks around questioning, insists, "Surely a condition like this *must* be treatable."

Finger-wagging Fern looks angrily at Mr. B.: "Now you are saying they are sick. One does not 'treat' well people. That is the attitude that cost me my son. Isn't the APA more qualified than we are to decide who is or is not sick?"

I step in to recommend Marcia Weitzman's *Homosexuality: As Viewed from Five Perspectives* and cite the part where she writes about several experts who deny the existence of empirical proof that Gay people have made the U-turn toward permanent change, just as non-Gay people have not been treated into changing their sexual identity. More important, I stress, is helping your Gay child to accept his or her Gayness as fact and to be assured of family love and support.

I refer to an interview with psychologist C.A. Tripp, Ph.D., author of *The Homosexual Matrix* and protégé of Kinsey, which has appeared in *New York* magazine. Asked about curing homosexuality, Dr. Tripp says:

Nobody could possibly cure homosexuality because the phenomena it comprises are not illnesses in the first place. A number of moralists and psychiatrists still claim to be able to change homosexuality, but whether that is ever possible depends on your criteria. If stopping the action is all that's meant, then joining a monastery or a nunnery might do it, or listening to Billy Graham and swearing off in the name of Jesus might work for a while. Or if "making a commitment to heterosexuality" is the criterion—Masters and Johnson demand this of their patients—then this sometimes "works" but only with people who have a degree of heterosexual response and who, by dint of will under the eyes of kindly authority figures, push their homosexual tastes aside. It all amounts to a bitter, desperate, tenuous hold on a forced heterosexuality.

I restate how Tripp points out that there has never been a validated case on record and strongly believes there never will be.

For a few minutes, the parents contemplate these words in silence. They are considering their options: take the kids as they are or in all likelihood lose them.

I suggest, "Maybe it's time to look at the issues we find most difficult to deal with."

Brick, putting his head in his hands, sighs. "I go crazy every time I think about what those girls do in bed together."

Fern, a retired schoolteacher, taking a sip of coffee, looks around the room. She addresses Brick's despair. She is exasperated.

"You have a married child. Do you think about what he does in bed? What are you—some kind of a voyeur? These kids are entitled to the same kind of privacy that non-Gays have."

Shelly, listening to Brick and Fern, comes back to her own family.

"I find I have a chip on my shoulder about them. I feel protective. They are mine and whoever hurts them deals with me. I've *had* time to get used to the idea. I feel guilty, of course. They were exposed to a battlefield at home. Maybe seeing what went on in our marriage turned them against man/woman relationships."

James, fumbling with the papers in front of him, interrupts. He is eager to get advice on his own problems.

"My daughter Barbara resents my pride in my successful son. She accuses me of feeling threatened as a man—you know, that male superiority thing. She says that because she finds women desirable, I find it a rejection of masculinity, and therefore of me. I squirm inside about this. She's probably right."

Our admonisher, Fern, pursing her lips and adjusting her eyeglasses, steps right in on that one.

"So have more contact. Reassure her. Lunch with her, too. Let her know that she has the same rights to be who she is as her brother has. Meet her friends. Take them out, too. She must feel belittled knowing that you jumped the hurdle with your son—that an achieving male can even be Gay. You have work to do on your relationship with her."

The others agree that James should look more deeply into his reasons for favoring his son and to recall in feelings and memory all that he loved in his daughter before he learned that she was Gay. They feel that it will also help the brother and sister to establish a closer relationship when they are released from being rivals for their father's attention and approval. "God knows," says one man, "they will certainly need each other after you are gone, both being Gay."

Mrs. A. asks the group what they think about her urging Marie to quit her job in Hollywood to live with her parents again.

The group turns to Mrs. A. and her husband. With relish, they gear themselves for a roasting. One woman says:

"Boy, are you ever selfish. You are facing old age and want to draw from her young strength—not to take care of her in her weakness."

Another parent blames the A.s' problems on the "empty nest syndrome."

"You got used to caring for a semi-invalid and can't
. accept her return to apparent good health and
independence. You're jealous of her lover and you
simply want to have your little girl back again.
You deny the issue of Lesbian caring and love—
the fact that these two women are establishing a
life together that is good for *them*."

Another participant who has been silent until now
jumps into the fray, saying that if Marie renounces
her Lesbianism and comes home to Mommy and
Daddy, they will be able to stave off old age, cra-
dling her again. They can feel like young parents once
again.

Mr. and Mrs. A. throw up their hands. "Is this
what you all think?"

As the A.'s look around the room, heads bob up
and down.

I think of how easy it is to be objective about other
people. This is perhaps an appropriate time to tell
them an anecdote about my best friend, Gwen, who
had found it easy to be objective about *my* son's
homosexuality:

"One day last spring, Gwen, who had been my ear
and shoulder throughout the first months of my
struggle to come to terms with Kenny's homosexuality, rang my doorbell. She was a widowed
friend of many years, and we had always confided in each other without reservation.'

"Gwen whispered, 'Guess what?'

"My ESP went to work. 'Leah's Gay?'

"'Oh, my God, yes. All the time you were up
and down about your feelings about Kenny, I was

saying to myself, "Thank God it's your kid and not mine." Someone up there must have been laughing at me. Leah told me that since her early teens, she has known that she was a Lesbian. Did Kenny know? Did you know?'

"I was defensive. 'No way. Don't you think I would have told you? Kenny never said a word about Leah.'

"Gwen rambled (reminding me of my own early reactions). 'I went through Brownie training for her...I bought pink clothes when she was a baby...she was always all girl...curls...long, dark eyelashes...she hates slacks—says they rape her...her singing voice is high and sweet...she plays the piano so beautifully...she gets a period ...it's impossible that she's Gay...there's nothing butch about Leah.' She was now crying and hysterical. 'I told her she must see a doctor.'

"I was annoyed. 'First of all, don't be an ass. Don't you think Lesbians menstruate?' She sounded too much like I did some years ago, and I took no pleasure in being reminded of that. Hearing Gwen parody me was like sitting in an echo chamber. Haunted, I reminded her of all the good advice she had pushed on me. 'So, it was all right for me to have a Gay child, but not for you.'

"Our friendship was teetering. She became defensive. 'Yes, it *is* all right for you. You're a flake anyway. I was raised with different values and I raised Leah the same way.'

"I replied coldly, 'Is this you or your crisis talking?' Gwen left without another word. An hour later she was back. We held each other tightly, laughing and crying. Gwen was once again able to laugh at herself—a quality I have always liked in her (and she in me).

"Today Gwen is knitting twin sweaters for

Leah and her sweetheart, Louise, who are snugly ensconced in an apartment eight blocks from Gwen in Queens. Leah and Louise have opened a gift shop together, and are involved in a close friendship with Gwen.

"I rhetorically ask the group, will this last? Maybe yes, maybe no. Most relationships are unpredictable—whether Gay or straight—but Gwen has been willing to accept the reality that her daughter is Gay and keep her most precious possession: Leah's love and good will."

The group laughs at the story, and the woman sitting next to me remarks that she wishes she could find humor in *her* situation. She supposes that in a few years and with some distance she may see the comic aspects of her daughter's Lesbianism. Wilma, who has been looking anxiously at her husband, asks:

"Has anyone here given some thought to my situation? After all, second marriages are par for the course. But how do I handle my son Teddy's relationship with his new stepfather, my worries about where he goes at night, what world he visits, where I cannot follow or understand. Help me, anyone."

The group is delighted to solve Wilma's problems. Advice flows. As it turned out, some of the suggestions were helpful, and Wilma did follow them. She had a long talk with Teddy, who revealed to her that his real father—from whom Wilma was divorced—had not found the boy's homosexuality problematic. It was agreed all around that the young man would live with his father and feel free to visit his mother and stepfather as he chose. She also arranged to see her son on a one-to-one basis frequently, thus giving herself more time to absorb all the new things in her life: more time to find out the meaning of Gay, to read, to learn, to work toward understanding. This was satisfactory to her present husband because he felt that Wilma was making an effort in behalf of their marriage. Of course, there was a long trek ahead, but Wilma did take the first steps toward arriving at some resolution in consideration of both her son and her husband. This stepfather situation reminds me of how I had been so relieved by Gene's immediate acceptance of Kenny's homosexuality that I never asked *why* at the time. Since then I had wondered—and told the group about Gene's reaction. Why wasn't he shocked about Kenny? Why was he so casual? I did not think about the reason at the time, but at a later date in a conversation at the Ortho meeting with my friend Harry Blumenfield, Assistant Director of Support Services of the Jewish Board of Guardians in New York, Harry found it curious that Gene was so agreeable about this idea of a homosexual stepson.

In turning it over, Harry suggested that as a stepfather Gene did not have the same investment in Kenny that his real father would have. When I told this to Gene, he said, "Maybe. Maybe if Kenny were my biological son, I'd have had some more work to do on myself."

Gene admitted that he had been perturbed by my edginess in the months following Kenny's coming out (to me), but he attributed it to problems in adjusting to each other and to the move. In fact, he wondered if our marriage was in trouble and if it was—why? On the day that I burst out that Kenny was Gay, Gene was immensely relieved that it was *only* that. So many things in life are relative!

In the case of Mr. and Mrs. B., Mrs. B. has already done an about-face since the last session and has had lunch with her Gay son and his "friend." She tells us that she had laughed for two hours with them. To her surprise, she found the "friend" personable and charming. However, a Thanksgiving holiday is approaching, and she is at a loss as to how to deal with an invitation to Nils and his "friend." Mr. B. is adamantly against it. Mrs. B. says that if they do not invite the "friend," their son stated flatly that he would not come at all. The couple lock horns over this, and I suggest that we pass over it until next week while they think about it and talk it over at home.

Mr. and Mrs. C., glancing at each other to see if they are still in agreement, cling to the conviction that their Gay son Mike had chosen this way of life to get back at his father for running in male prostitutes in his work as a detective. The C.'s say that their son had always rebelled—he refused to go in for team sports such as Little League—and that was his way of defying his father and what counted in his father's eyes. Mrs. B., dabbing at her eyes with a Kleenex, says:

"I must believe that this is his temporary choice. I believe that what he chose he can choose to turn away from. How can he not expect us to be bitter when he reviles everything we hold dear?"

Mrs. B. and her husband are agitated about how to explain the situation to family and friends. Mrs. B. reaches for another Kleenex:

"I'm most bothered about the obvious Gay ones, as I said last week—the ones who flaunt it. I just cannot deal with that."

Fern stands up and puts her hands on her hips. In her deep smoker's voice, she grates:

"So you not only put down your Gay son and his friends, but you put down women. Your attitude stems from looking down at what is feminine—womanly. Why? Why should it not be a compliment to women that some of your son's friends choose to swish and sway, admitting the girly part of them? I thought this was the time of women coming into their own? Why should it be so unbearable if some young Gay men mince a bit? Who do they hurt? And if they hurt you, you had better look deep down to find out why it bothers you so. Women who feel that way don't think much of their own sex or themselves. And the men who feel that way certainly show where they're at in their opinion of women and their doubts about themselves."

Resting her case, Fern sits quietly for the rest of the session. Some of the men cast dagger eyes at her, but she turns her gaze away, her eyes narrowed into slits.

A woman asks Gerry how she is doing. Her problem—coming to terms with the metamorphosis of her son's sexual identity—overwhelms most of us. As the group eyes Gerry curiously and compassionately, she begins:

"Gloria referred me to a group called Confide and suggested that I write to the Janus Information Facility for further recommendations. [Confide works with transsexuals and their families but not families alone.*] I do feel that I am thawing somewhat. I'm not as anesthetized. It is comforting listening to all of you coming out of your own closets little by little."

*I later also referred Gerry for private therapy.

Mr. and Mrs. D. voice their homophobia again. Mrs. D. says that she cannot permit her daughter Elinor to display affection in her house to a girlfriend, even so far as holding hands, but that her son had every right to manifest his feelings openly for his girlfriends.

Fern visibly gnashes her teeth at that one, but one of the group members holds her back and tells her that her opinions are monopolizing our time. Fern shrugs, annoyed, and sits back.

Mrs. B. then asks Mrs. D. what her younger children think of the situation. Mrs. D. says the fact that they do not know about their sister's Lesbianism and she will not permit them to know is another cause of dissension between herself and Elinor.

> "My younger kids horse around. They call each other 'fag' when they fight. They don't have to get upset by what my daughter says that she is."

Mrs. D. looks stricken. So does Mr. D. A woman says, "Where did they hear the word *fag*?"

"Probably from us."

"Oh."

Mr. D. admits that *anyone* crossing established boundaries—racial, religious *or* sexual—makes him extremely uncomfortable.

> "I feel comfortable when we all have a niche, and I feel good about my own niche. My religion, one of these niches, is a comfort. Accepting differences has always been difficult for me."

One of the men comments that if Mr. D. wants to keep in contact with Elinor he had better crack down on the language he permits at home which disparages a minority group. The man adds that he recalls that

Mr. D. has said that he will probably "get used to all this in time."

> "You probably will get more used to the idea just from coming to the workshop and talking about your feelings. Probably as we get more and more into it, it will be less and less unknown to us. Maybe the myths will go away and real people— our children—will take their place."

Mr. G., again holding his wife's hand, recounts the first time he suspected that his daughter might be Gay.

> "Jane had invited another girl for dinner when she was in high school, and I noticed how she looked at this girl, hanging on her every word. It was as lovesick a look as I have ever seen. It disturbed me, and I wondered what lay ahead for my girl, but then years later, when she 'conformed,' as she now puts it, by marrying, having children and running a lovely home, I decided that she had been passing through the girlish-crush stage. My wife refuses to meet with her—uh, woman friend, which distresses my daughter. But Jane has always been respectful. She honors her mother's wishes. We're Greek and the filial devotion and respect to family elders is ingrained in us. We're worried about the effect of all this on our grandchildren. It's difficult to see them when *that woman* is there, so special meetings have to be arranged. That's awkward. We were used to seeing the kids frequently and informally. We love our son-in-law and we miss him."

Mrs. G. adds that she firmly believes that the other—uh, woman—has led Jane astray. At this point,

Mr. and Mrs. G. are at an impasse, but are opening up. They are questioning—and indicting, to be sure—but at least they are talking. For the first time, their closet door is creaking. They are pushing it open—just a crack.

Now as we near the end of our session, the tensions dissolve—a little. A trust has been established among the participants as they realize they share a central theme: the commonality of Gay children. A feeling of relief is generated as words tumble. *Heads nod: Yes, I know, I've been there. I've felt this. Me too.*

As we prepare to leave, I observe to the group that we parents have had no role models to show us the way. In a sense we feel as isolated as our children felt when they grew to realize they were Gay—as though we had been pushed out to sea on an ice floe. Who has been there for us? Not the culture. Not the government. Not the clergy. We need to find our own way with little help from the outside world. We are on our own.

That night, I wrote a long entry in my Workshop Journal.

Parents fire away all sorts of pressing questions. Whether to tell spouse or sibling. I say secrecy usually bad idea, creates an emotionally unhealthy conspiracy in the family. Despite the initial pain, parents should support each other in this crisis. Sharing knowledge may bring the couple to closer, more intimate relationship. I tell group that in his practice as a clinical psychologist, Kenny sees this situation often. Says when one parent knows and other does not, one in the dark feels—unconsciously—left out, detached and psychologically lonely. Sharing knowledge can help bridge that gap.

Kenny voices similar sentiments about coming

out to a sibling. Veil of secrecy permeates the spontaneity and honesty of family life.

Still, Gay person right in the final analysis to decide. Must bear in mind that if only one family member is informed a lonely burden placed upon the shoulders of the confidant.

Always selectivity and prudence in order when certain circumstances in the family prevail and disclosure would wreak havoc on intrafamilial relationships. But by and large, sooner family knows, the whole nuclear family, sooner they can begin to deal with it until it gains proper perspective.

The question of cause rippled through the meeting over and over. I repeat, no known proven cause. We are here to deal with the reality of what is, not why. I cited readings on this. Must release ourselves of guilt—stop hugging it to our bosoms. Not much fun, feeling guilty. Not warranted.

The question of cure.

Again, discuss findings of respected experts. Cure implies restoration to health and soundness.

What to tell relatives, friends and neighbors? I quote Kenny: "This is a difficult question because it implies that parents are obliged to recite a historical anthropology of their children's lives. This is usually not the case, and rarely do people with sensitivity and manners come right out and ask, 'Is Johnny Gay?' If you as a family member are not yet comfortable with your child's sexual orientation (NOTE: Do not use the word preference*), then be true to yourself and do not discuss it publicly. Defer, deflect, demur; don't discourse. Introduce your child and his lover as 'John and his friend Sam.' Neither convention nor external pressure demand further explanation until you are ready and willing with selected, trusted friends.*

You always have the right to say no. Over time you should be able to make a healthy adaptation."

If you liked, loved your child before proclamation, you will probably gain more respect for him/her afterward. Deepening respect will communicate itself to those you choose to tell about his/her sexual orientation. Listener might just admire you (even though reluctantly) for having gone so far in your personal growth.

Perceptions? We hardly went delving. Preconceived notions apparent in body language: pursed lips, turned-down mouths, hunched shoulders, frowns. General acquiescence that homosexuality was definitely out of bounds for the likes of their children.

Problems? Issues? The most prevalent pangs felt by the parents that Gay children did not and would not meet their expectations. As parents, we usually dreamed of more for our children—more than we had, or at least as much. More affluence, more recognition, more success, more joy (and as Kenny observed)—ironically, better relationships with their parents (us) than we had with ours.

Parents have mapped course for their kids to live life successfully as defined by them. Now suffering rude awakening. Their children had shattered these dreams. Not just acting out true feeling quietly, but out in the open.

Fears about children's physical safety and social acceptance. Regrets for manner they handled confrontations. Self-doubts about the part they may have played in the development of their children's sexuality. Apprehension about the effect on a stepparent or a sibling. Religious concerns. Denial child really Gay. Maybe subject to lure of lover! Horrified speculation about manner child makes love.

So far, the parents were caught up in own feelings: not yet wondering how it had been for kids. Next week, Dr. Patrick Murphy.

Week III: Historical Overview

The parents talk animatedly with each other as they arrange themselves for our third session. While we wait for the latecomers, I distribute copies of "Changing Views of Homosexuality" by Elizabeth Ogg (Public Affairs Pamphlet #563) and the introduction to *Positively Gay: New Approaches in Gay Life*, edited by Betty Berzon, Ph.D., and Robert Leighton (Celestial Arts):

> I frequently think about the positive contributions that homosexuals make to society. Our democratic system believes strongly in pluralism. In a pluralistic society, individuals and minorities are valued highly. I believe that the gay minority is the last minority to finally begin receiving the recognition it deserves for the many creative contributions it makes....
>
> What I look forward to and what I hope this book will help accomplish is to show the gay community that as important as sexuality is, it is also the most unimportant thing. A lot of people will disagree with me and I know it. I should preface this by saying that I have led a very active sexual life, a full sexual life. Sexuality to me is one of the most recreative experiences when it is good, when it is with someone one loves, of any experience in life....
>
> Despite that, I still say that what keeps some gay persons from growing is that they get locked into this prison of defining themselves as first of all gay, meaning that they focus on sexuality and how

to get sexual gratification. Therefore, the richness of life—within the gay community and related to non-gay people—passes them by.... They are victims of themselves really. The attitudes are out there, of course, but many gay people have allowed themselves to be imprisoned by those attitudes. They focus on being gay, being different, being outcasts, being ostracized.... The tragedy is that they are cutting themselves off from many people who might be sources of extended or rich relationships in which they can expand and grow....

It is equally important for straight people to realize that by stereotyping gay people, by not knowing what gays are really like, by not having the privilege of knowing gays and having them as friends, they too are depriving themselves....

While the parents were absorbing this material, I handed out a list of prominent Gay people throughout history taken from *The People's Almanac Presents the Book of Lists* by D. Wallechinsky, I. Wallace and A. Wallace (New York: William Morrow and Company, 1977).

Women

Sappho (flourished c. 600 B.C.),
  Greek poet
Christine (1626–1689),
  Swedish queen
Madame de Stael (1766–1817),
  French author
Charlotte Cushman (1816–1876),
  U.S. actress
Gertrude Stein (1874–1946),
  U.S. author
Alice B. Toklas (1877–1967),
  U.S. author-cook
Virginia Woolf (1882–1941),
  British author
Victoria Sackville-West
  (1892–1962), British author

Bessie Smith (1894–1937),
  U.S. singer
Kate Millett (b. 1934,)
  U.S. author
Janis Joplin (1943–1970),
  U.S. singer

Men

Zeno of Elea (fifth century B.C.),
  Greek philosopher
Sophocles (496–406 B.C.),
  Greek playwright
Euripides (480–406 B.C.),
  Greek dramatist
Socrates (470?–399 B.C.),
  Greek philosopher
Aristotle (384–322 B.C.),
  Greek philosopher

Alexander the Great
(356–323 B.C.),
Macedonian ruler
Julius Caesar (100–44 B.C.),
Roman emperor
Hadrian (76–138 A.D.),
Roman emperor
Richard the Lion Hearted
(1157–1199), British king
Richard II (1367–1400),
British king
Sandro Botticelli (1444?–1510),
Italian painter
Leonardo da Vinci (1452–1519),
Italian painter-scientist
Julius III (1487–1555),
Italian pope
Benvenuto Cellini (1500–1571),
Italian goldsmith
Francis Bacon (1561–1626),
British philosopher
Christopher Marlowe (1564–1593),
British playwright
James I (1566–1625),
British king
John Milton (1608–1674),
British author
Jean-Baptiste Lully (1637–1687),
French composer
Peter the Great (1672–1725),
Russian czar
Frederick the Great (1712–1786),
Prussian king
Gustavus III (1746–1792),
Swedish king
Alexander von Humboldt
(1769–1859), German naturalist
George Gordon, Lord Byron
(1788–1824), British poet
Hans Christian Andersen
(1805–1875), Danish author
Walt Whitman (1819–1892),
U.S. poet

Horatio Alger (1832–1899),
U.S. author
Samuel Butler (1835–1902),
British author
Algernon Swinburne (1837–1909),
British poet
Peter Ilyich Tchaikovsky
(1840–1893), Russian composer
Paul Verlaine (1844–1896),
French poet
Arthur Rimbaud (1854–1900),
French poet
Oscar Wilde (1854–1900),
British playwright
Frederick Rolfe (Baron Corvo)
(1860–1913), British author
Andre Gide (1869–1951),
French author
Marcel Proust (1871–1922),
French author
E. M. Forster (1879–1970),
British author
John Maynard Keynes
(1883–1946), British economist
Harold Nicholson (1886–1968),
British author-diplomat
T. E. Lawrence (1888–1935),
British soldier-author
Jean Cocteau (1889–1963),
French author
Waslaw Nijinksy (1890–1950),
Russian ballet dancer
Bill Tilden (1893–1953),
U.S. tennis player
Christopher Isherwood (b. 1904),
British author
Dag Hammarskjold (1905–1961),
Swedish U.N. secretary-general
W. H. Auden (1907–1973),
British-U.S. poet
Jean Genet (b. 1910),
French playwright

Tennessee Williams (1911–1983),
U.S. playwright
Merle Miller (b. 1919),
U.S. author
Pier Paolo Pasolini (1922–1975),
Italian film director
Brendan Behan (1923–1964),
Irish author

Malcolm Boyd (b. 1923),
U.S. theologian
Allan Ginsberg (b. 1926),
U.S. poet
David Bowie (b. 1947),
British singer

I recommend *Gay American History*, by Jonathan Katz, which places the struggle for Gay liberation in a historical context and ties the existence of Gays into the American dream. I also recommend Vito Russo's *The Celluloid Closet*, a biting account of homosexuality in the movies, where the Gay person—never heroic—comes off as loser or villain.

Although a few parents express keen interest in hearing the historical overview I plan, most prefer to discuss exactly what troubles them right now. In a previous workshop, one of our guests, Emery Hetrick, M.D., a noted Gay psychiatrist, clinical assistant professor of psychiatry at New York University Medical Center and president of the Institute for the Protection of Lesbian and Gay Youth, took us from biblical and classical times through early and medieval Christian, Renaissance and Victorian times to our own era of rapidly changing attitudes. That was the session when Dr. Hetrick told the parents, *"Homosexuality is not a form of misbehavior. It is not a deliberate choice. It is a discovery."*

At another workshop, our guest was Terry Miller, a novelist/playwright. When he was asked what it was like to grow up Gay in a Long Island suburb, he said he had been unaware of it consciously. He saw the world of romance in screen, family and advertising as an abstract depicting only men and women in love—never people of the same sex. Even though *his* family was extremely liberal and he had nothing to rebel against, he repressed his homosexual thoughts. Limits set by the outside world were tremendously disturbing to him. He told us how he simply did not identify with what he saw in the public display of heterosexual love. Therefore, he restrained conscious feelings of homosexuality until his early twenties when he emerged to himself and others as Gay.

Then there was the night that Nan and her lover Cindy, two Gay teachers, attended a session as our guest speakers.

Neither young woman fit the dyke stereotype of female homosexuality. Rather, they were chic, attractive, ebullient. Both are divorced. Both are mothers. Both, having denied their Lesbian tendencies, had come out to themselves when they were thirty. When the feelings about other women kept bobbing up, they realized that they could no longer push them down. Nan told her husband of nine years that she was Gay after she knew that she loved Cindy and could not continue her deception as a married woman. Surprisingly to Nan, her husband, although shocked, admitted that he had felt something missing in their marriage—a kind of basic emptiness of response. After penetratingly honest talks, they agreed to let each other go. They worked out an equitable arrangement to share custody of the children. But Nan's parents were frantic when they were told the reason for the break up. However, as the months went by and they saw how right she seemed with Cindy and how devoted the two women were to each other, they gradually began to yield. They listened to how their daughter really felt about herself and made honest efforts to understand. Their home is open to the two women where they are now received as a couple.

Cindy, however, had a more trying time. She thought long and hard about the letter she finally wrote to her husband revealing herself as Gay, saying at the end of five pages that "the fact is, dear Ray, I'm Gay." When a woman in the group asked Cindy how he took this news, Cindy's eyes just rolled back, looking up, which said it all. Cindy did not go in to detail about her custody arrangement, but it was apparently far from satisfactory to her. "But, I am happier with Nan than I have ever been," she assured us. "At least, I'm no longer living a lie."

We discussed the adjustment their children must make. The difficulties that lie ahead. But then, we reasoned, children have always been subject to the ways of the world: wars, bombings, divorce, death—so many trials. And now, many children must cope with being the child of a Gay parent. Cindy emphasized her view: that a loving parent of any sexual orientation, who has sound moral values, would help children to find their way. Of course, she noted, society could be more helpful. One of the men scratched his head and said that when he thinks about the state of his own tumultuous marriage, maybe the girls were on to something.

Noticing the openmouthed, wide-eyed expressions on the faces of most of the group, I saw that looking at Gay parenting is incomprehensible to parents who are still trying to understand their childrens' homosexuality. But the parents certainly got a preview of things to come: that is, that some of them would surely become grandparents through their Gay children. But we were not crossing that bridge yet.

The parents fired questions with machine-gun rapidity at Nan and Cindy. "How did you feel growing up? When did you know? Are you worried that your children will be Gay?"

The womens' answers conveyed a sense of courage and determination. They would make their lives work and try to teach their children sensitivity and tolerance. And they hoped that their children would be allowed to reach their full human potential, no matter what their orientation.

One man considered how much simpler life would have been for Gay children had they had sex education in school from early on, which would have included information about homosexuality. Forthright information.

Tonight, however, we have a different guest: muscular, redhaired Dr. Patrick Murphy—a professor in the department of social sciences at a local university.

Dr. Murphy is an overt Gay activist and talks about the lack of role models for young Gay people. He tells us how alien and isolated they feel in a world that beats the drum for heterosexual activity only; how helpful it would be for them to grow up knowing that there are others like them. Everywhere. (I notice that some of the women eye Dr. Murphy wistfully. One woman whispers to me that our guest looks like a young Van Heflin. Both of us are old enough to remember Van Heflin. "So this is where the creme de la creme has gone," she only half jokes.) He tells us about the different levels of familial acceptance; how the doors of understanding will open wider and wider as time goes by and the families *work* at understanding. He reveals to us that he has been with one man for ten years and that steadfastness is a "noncategorized statistic" not generally attributed to Gay people. We hear that long-term relationships between Gay people are just as usual as they are between non-Gay people.

A woman shares with us that finally, after ten years of keeping the fact of her son's homosexuality secret, she has called three close friends who live in California and revealed to them that her son is Gay. "I feel so unburdened now," she says. Dr. Murphy comments that this is not unusual—that parents often find it easier to share such knowledge at a safe distance when they first come out of their closets.

When the expected question of *why* these children

are Gay pops up again and again, the professor repeats what so many experts say: that it has *never* been proven as to why people are Gay or non-Gay.

Another woman complains that her thirty-year-old daughter accepts complete financial support from her mother and older female lover. Dr. Murphy points out that many Gay children feel unsure about how to deal with Gay maturity—an unknown and complex state of being. So they put off growing up a bit longer, clinging to youthful dependency. Its safer to stay a child and hold on to childish dependency until they have reached a more confident stage of development. But with the encouragement of those close to them and in the course of their own growth, he feels that they will develop independence.

Dr. Murphy leaves to attend another meeting.

We continue with last week's examination of our struggles to accept homosexuality in our sons and daughters: the main issues are how to tell friends and family, whether or not to include them in family cele- brations, the effeminacy of some Gay men, the role of grandparents and the use of detractive language at home.

Brick looks around and says what he is to say at every session.

"I still say that I would rather be anywhere else but here, but I do feel better about the whole thing when I leave.

"Now here's a zinger for the group. Amy resents the big party we chipped in for when our son got engaged. She wants the same. And gifts. Amy and her sweetie purchased a big house in Seattle. They each got promotions with one of the Seven Sister oil companies. Big jobs. They want us to celebrate their success with all of our friends and relatives. Their straight and Gay friends in Seattle have thrown them a party. I think it's also some sort of anniversary for them. What do they want of me? How can I take over my club for such a party? What can I tell my buddies? And their wives? My wife and I are going crazy with this."

Brick holds out his hands, palms up, shrugging after each question. Everyone shouts at once, voices shrill with advice. Censorious.

"Some nerve! What about *our* traditions? Those Japs! Give them a finger, they want an arm! I'd give her a party—a one-way ticket to the Yucatan!"

The group becomes quarrelsome. I ask for quiet. They simmer down. Wilma, her eyes brimming and her jaw tight, says slowly and thoughtfully:

"Just think. Think about how these kids have gone through all this alone. Growing up—alone. Alone with the brothers and sisters and parents and aunts and uncles. Never being able to be themselves or to talk to us. Any of us. Knowing that they were going to be ostracized, shut out or hurried off to psychiatrists if they dared open their mouths about who they really were. Can you imagine what it must have been like for them? Feeling alien in their own homes? With their own families? Growing up is lonely and frightening enough, but growing up Gay must have been shattering to their sense of who they were. We have been so taken up with *our* own hurts and disappointment in them. How about *their* hurt?"

Wilma's eyes mist over:

"I was his mother and I was not there for him. He had to grow up to be six feet tall before he could *tell me the truth* about himself."

Fern, who can identify with Wilma's sorrow about her son's isolation, understands what both parents and their Gay children need:

> "Sure. Sure they want what their brothers and sisters have. They don't want to be deprived and shuttered away. There are ways of honoring them without spelling it out."

Brick, ever concerned (as most parents are) with what his friends and neighbors will think of them, asks, "How?"

Fern, sensible and direct, explains to Brick:

> "Celebrate Amy. Celebrate *them*. You can say that Amy and her friend have just bought a home with their own money that they earned from important jobs that they hold. You *feel* like giving a party for them. Period. Invite who you like. You do not have to translate their relationship. People will have figured it out anyway. The ones who come will have fun. Most people don't need an excuse to party."

Shelly, turning to me, brings up a similar dilemma she had faced concerning her daughter Carmen:

> "When I received an invitation to a shower for Carmen and her lover for their new apartment, at first I decided not to go. But at the last minute I changed my mind. They served coffee and cake and opened the presents for their new apartment. I'm glad that I changed my mind. They were so happy to see me. I sort of legitimatized them. Amy and her lover say that they had and have no role models. Neither do we as parents. We have to follow our feelings and do what is comfortable for us. Some of my friends were appalled that I

went to the shower. Some said that I was gutsy. But I wanted to share the moment with Carmen. The step that Carmen took in setting up housekeeping with a woman she cares for in front of her whole little world. I was not sorry. Yet, I still squirm at their humor, their outlook. It's so foreign to mine. But my options are small. Take her as she is or lose her. I'm taking her."

Brick, still thinking about his own problem, looks expectant. He hopes one of us will have a solution. I offer some thoughts.

"Brick, if you are comfortable with the idea of giving a party for your daughter and her friend, then do it. Your genuine friends will come. Others may not. So they will talk about you. You know that old adage, 'Sticks and stones...' But, if you have not yet reached that degree of comfort, but you want to do something equal to what you have done for your son, give them a terrific gift. Treat them to a trip or just have an elegant intimate dinner for them inviting your closest friends who are aware of the situation. The girls are not the ones to call the shots here. You have the right to proceed at your own pace. It has taken them time to act upon their departure from the traditional. You have the right to take the time you need to depart from what is traditional for you. Without listening to your own insides, you and your wife cannot act from the outside with honesty and sincerity."

James looks at me with irritation.

"Gloria, I cannot believe that you are all that accepting of homosexuality. I did not come here to listen to sermons."

Brick, who by now is completely at home in the workshop and apparently protective of me, jumps in:

"Don't project *your* feelings on to Gloria. If she has arrived at a certain place with all of this, let her stay there. We all know that it took her more than twenty minutes."

I turn quickly to Mr. and Mrs. A.: "So what is happening with Marie in Hollywood?"

Mrs. A., intently listening, speaks up:

"It appears that Marie is not about to retire with us to Florida or from her life-style. Of course, we don't want to lose contact. That is why we are here. We called her and set up arrangements for a two-week visit to California. Marie insists that we stay in their home. We agreed."

When Mrs. A. emits a long-suffering sigh, I am reminded of a recent play Gene and I saw where a character had said that sighs are indicative of old people. I say that was a positive step for both of them and I express the hope that during the course of the visit they will look for the positive and joyous in their daughter's life. And enjoy the visit to boot. However, the A.'s just look resigned. A kind of if-you-can't-change-it-go-with-it resignation.

Mrs. B. says, "Well, we have compromised about inviting Nils and his friend for Thanksgiving."

Seeing that the B.'s are moving a step forward in their ability to communicate with their son, I ask, "How's that?"

Mrs. B. answers, "He's coming as a friend from 'out-of-town.' Incognito."

Both the B.'s look at us defiantly, their eyes saying, "Unfair? Perhaps, but it's the best we can do now."

Congratulating the B.'s on their move, I tell them at least they are going in a new direction toward their son—something they were unable to do two weeks ago. They have opened the doors of their home. They have proceeded a few inches. Inviting the Gay couple for a holiday dinner is a measure of a modicum of success in this couple's wobbly but change-directed attitude in viewing their son as a Gay person who is also the other half of a couple. I fall into another sermon about how parents cannot expect to do an about-face in attitude overnight. They must proceed at their own pace. That they are working on it is what counts.

Mr. and Mrs. C. still have the outlook, "Convince us. Just try."

Many parents continue to be troubled by the "effeminacy" of some Gay men. One of the men says that he can accept his *son's* homosexuality, but he cannot accept his son's friends.

"I know it isn't fashionable, but I can't bear those *Nelly* types. If they choose to act this way, they should take the consequences. We're here because we thought we could help our son turn away from what we feel is his choice. We just can't live with this life-style."

Another father thinks he has arrived at a sort of token acceptance of his son's homosexuality. As long as his son does not flaunt it, he can live with it. He tells this story:

"So, I invited my son and his—uh, pal—to my tennis club. I swallowed hard when I saw this 'friend' flit around the court. This guy dipped before he served, gave the ball a little slap at what he considered was a cross-court shot and practically arabesqued into a backhand. All this, plus one earring. My son can 'pass.' But this character— never. I don't care if I come off here as sounding like a hypocrite. I'm not that liberated yet to carry off a scene like that nonchalantly. That's why I'm here. I have a hell of a time with the twinkie types. My friends cocked their heads much too cutely and asked me who my 'lovely' guest was. I usually have an answer for anything, but I was floored. How do I handle this? *I don't want it to show!*"

He looks at me in defiance. I try not to sermonize but I do.

"Different people have different levels of security about how they appear to the world. Your feelings are not unusual, and probably many people in this room go along with you. I am sure that it does give straight people quite a turn to see a blatantly overt Gay fellow in their midst on their private turf. They are simply not used to it. It takes time to be able to lift an eyebrow back at others. Some people are never comfortable enough with themselves to be able to do it. You will decide how far along you can go with this in time."

Similarly, I was reminded of a recent incident where I, too, had beaten a retreat for a few seconds. I told the group how when Sam and Kenny were visiting us in the country and were out fishing on the lake, two Gay friends of theirs stopped by en route from their vacation. When the young men arrived—handsome, tanned, brawny—I walked them down to our dock to point out the boat the boys were using. As it came into view, one of the tawny, muscled fellows jumped up and down excitedly, spotting Ken and Sam in their boat and yelling, "Yoo-hoo! Yoo-hoo!" His voice pierced the quiet of the lakefront. I found myself coloring and darted nervous looks at some nearby sunbathers. But the moment passed. Quickly. I was once again enjoying their company. Later that evening, Kenny—tongue-in-cheek—suggested that we all see a movie together. "That is," said Kenny, "if Gene doesn't mind being seen with four flaming queens." Gene replied blithely that it would be okay *if* no one bothered him while he was driving.

It takes time, and it does take getting used to. Coming to terms with the fact of a Gay child is an ever-ongoing process.

Wilma suggests that the son bring more neutral-looking and -acting friends the next time. Another woman says:

> "Take them to Central Park to play tennis. Why should you have to explain to your friends when you haven't explained to yourself yet."

Another woman, who had only spoken to tell us about her difficulty in accepting her daughter's Lesbianism, says:

> "Maybe in time. Maybe in time, it won't matter. Maybe we'll all get used to it one of these days. After all, our kids should be more important than what other people think."

The father who has difficulty with "flaunting" says that maybe he will just see his son and his friends at home or in a restaurant for a while until he gets more used to the whole idea (muttering under his breath), "If I ever do."

I have recently discussed parental consternation over effeminacy and butchiness in their Gay children with Jim Saslow, former New York editor of the Gay newspaper, *The Advocate.* Jim suggests that people examine what they are really resisting. Do they realize that there are no longer strict rules about what was once considered normal? Do they realize that the percentage of Americans living in nuclear families is getting smaller and smaller? Assume that parents are resisting letting friends and neighbors know—perhaps they should see this in the light of its not being their problem but the problem of the friends and neighbors. The world is changing. Parents of Gay children who want to keep the relationship going must adapt. To accept that the child is what he or she is. "Perhaps it's time to chuck some preconceptions about 'appropriate behavior,'" says Jim. On the other side of the coin, Jim feels that the Gay children can accommodate themselves to more "appropriate" behavior, too, when in the company of their parents—that the children need *not* inflame parents unnecessarily.

One father points out that this couple knew the slant of the workshop when they registered. Perhaps they are challenging their own precepts using us as their conduit. Perhaps they are looking to be overruled. Twenty-odd eyebrows knitted. We then turn to the anxious grandparents in our midst. They still had not met with their daughter's lover and kept putting it off. Having taken a position of inflexibility, they are also attempting to save face. But they sorely miss seeing their grandchildren and are hurting at being at odds with this daughter.

James proposes that the couple meet with the daughter and her lover on neutral ground such as her office or the father's office over a cup of coffee. It would not encourage intimacy such as the coziness of meeting at their homes, but will still establish an initial contact. Mr. G. likes the idea. His wife vetoes it. The following exchange takes place:

"Suppose I meet with them on my own first?"
"Without me?" (Spousal rebellion!)
"We can't go on like this. I miss the kids. I miss our daughter. We are cutting off our noses."

James, who has been coming to grips with his relationships with his Gay son and daughter, is able now to see the other person's problems more clearly.

"You miss the point. You are the ones objecting. You are the ones who have to water down these objections. She is Gay to stay. You have to accept this and work with it."
"All right," Mrs. G. replies but says to her husband, "You go first."

I then discuss grandparents.

"Grandparents, who usually haven't the same investment in the children as the parents, simply want to enjoy the renewed youth around them and the promise of that youth. What mattered so much yesterday has receded in importance today.
"They made certain mistakes with their children. If they are aware of this, they want to lean forward and hold out their hand to the grandchild. The grandchild brings life back into their lives. Grandparents usually carry a wallet full of pictures of grandchildren—something they did not do when they were bringing up their own children. When they do this, people often yawn aloud and groan inwardly.
"I am leading up to the fact that many grandparents I have either spoken to or heard about replied, "So?" when they were informed about a Gay grandchild.
"When I was invited to appear on the WNYC

Senior Edition radio show last fall, some of us in the studio were quite teary when a quivery voice phoned in her story. She said that her young grandson visited her regularly in a room that she had near her family, and that they were very close. 'One day he said to me, "Grandma, I have something to tell you. If you find it unbearable, just tell me so and I'll walk out and close the door behind me and never bother you again. I am a homosexual."

"I said, 'Dear boy. I love you now and I'll love you always. Please, don't ever close that door.'

"This is not to say that there are not inflexible grandparents or grandparents unable to deal with such a revelation, for whatever reason."

I tell the group that perhaps it is timely to recall the words of George Orwell in *1984* when his protagonist says he remembers a time "... when members of a family stood by one another without needing to know the reason."

One of the parents asks me about Kenny's grandparent. I tell them about my own eighty-three-year-old mother's reaction to Kenny:

"My eighty-three-year-old mother finally asked outright whether or not Kenny was homosexual. Recently widowed, she had time to think about this question for quite a while. Her reaction to my 'Yes, he is' was 'Oh. Couldn't he curb it?' 'Ma, he is not a puppy—he is a young man.' I was defensive. She thought a moment, then said, 'Well. Both Kenny and Sam are very special young men as far as I'm concerned.' She had seen the bedroom they both share when they hosted the family at Thanksgiving two years earlier. She had seen the house they had built together—the investment and the commitment. She had seen that neither Sam nor Kenny were dating women. Finally, she spoke about what she had strongly suspected. Yet my mother does waiver in her acceptance. Sometimes she seems totally accepting, but then may lecture Kenny on the telephone about keeping a low profile. She tells him he has worked long and hard to attain his Ph.D. and that he must protect himself professionally. At other times I get calls and mailings from her about a television program (a Gay granny is the latest) about Gay issues or a mailing of a news article about yet another injustice being meted out to Gay people. These injustices inflame her. Her consciousness is gradually going up and up, and her interest in the subject is mounting. Now she is personally involved. What happens to Gay people happens to one of her favorite grandsons. (It was Sam and Kenny who helped move my parents when they moved into a senior citizens' apartment house last year.)

"She keeps in touch with Kenny and Sam. Certainly my mother has a distance to go, for this is a new and strange way of life to her. But she is willing to learn—and I believe that she will. Even at eighty-three."

The group is astonished by my mother's resiliency. Then I tell about a client:

"I have an eighty-year-old client who had wisely blended his Lesbian daughter and her mate unselfconsciously into the family years before this subject became so topical. Today, as a widower, he enjoys a close and comforting living arrangement with both of them. They insist that he accompany them to their summer place on Long

Island where he is known as 'Pop' to all their friends.

"As opposed to this man is another client—an embittered seventy-nine-year-old woman who did the 'never-darken-my-door-again' routine with her Lesbian daughter and has lived to rue the day. The daughter is now a top executive in a prestigious firm. Although her father was a bank president and well connected, both parents were adamant about not helping her, either financially, socially or emotionally. She worked it all through alone. Which is just what she tells her now-widowed mother. 'I have confidence in you, Ma. You'll work things through on your own.' That is, when they talk on the telephone, which is twice a year."

We are running late again—it is time to go. The group starts to gather up their coats and file out in their usual clusters of twos, threes and fours to continue their deliberations at coffee shops or bars. I am left to smile apologetically at the impatient drama group gathered in the hall. On the subway going home, I think of the man who has "not come to listen to sermons." Certainly I never intend to sermonize. How can I, of all people, preach?

By no means am I the consistently enlightened shepherd attempting to lead a flock all the time. Some of the parents stir up my old doubts. Old devils dance. I have to jolt myself back to reality several times. Coming to terms with Gay children is a never-ending battle. However sanguine we may feel one day has nothing to do with the undercurrents stirred up in us another day. I think of my lapses. There have been times when I would notice Kenny talking animatedly to a pretty girl. I would perk up and say, "That's a pretty girl." Exasperated, Kenny would accuse me of not having "worked him out." I would back off sheepishly. A chance remark—almost anything, a news article, a film, a speech—may throw our complacency to the lions. Then we must wend our way back on course, back to restating what we have learned. And believing it. It is continually reassuring, however, to see the vast numbers of emerging Gay people give us parents the backbone to swim against the tide.

When I arrive home, I write the following entry in my Workshop Journal:

Dr. Murphy sheds illumination on the way our children must have felt, growing up atypical, how some kids hold on to childlike dependency because they don't know how to be grown-up Gays. Safer to stay a child longer. Relief one member felt when calling close friends out West to talk about Gay son. Says she attributes this directly to new strengths she is building at workshop. Another parent considering choices about entertaining Gay daughter and lover. Funny how most parents avoid the word lover. (I can't think of an appropriate alternative except friend.*)*

Some probe deeply into the years our Gay children had endured without communicating difference to anyone. Felt frightened, in danger and apart. Tears shed in workshop over what kids went through. Glimmers of awareness of what they had to bear seeping into consciousness. Others believe kids' Gayness just "nastiness" to torment parents. Personally I feel these rigid parents are playing devil's advocate—daring us to convince them that it's all right to be Gay. Give reasons. Show facts. Disprove outside world's condemnations. Prove them all wrong. Was that the message my social worker's third ear is hearing? An auditory mirage? Maybe not.

Two couples move toward meeting child's lover—

*one at Gay child's home, the other on less intimate
territory. At last dealing with hows and wheres of
coming together.*

*Remember to photocopy pages of William Sloane
Coffin's sermon, and article on Jewish and Protes-
tant views of Gayness for next session's "Getting
Philosophical."*

Remember to photocopy quote from Counselling
Lesbian Women and Gay Men, *by Moses and Hawkins,
Jr., (C.V Mosby Co., 1982) for those who are concerned
about role-taking and sterotypes.**

Week IV: Getting Philosophical

I open the session with a review of our discoveries
about homosexuality. Our Gay children are polymor-
phic. They come in all colors, shapes and sizes; they
are athletic and nonathletic, artistic and nonartistic,
musical and nonmusical; good-looking and plain; bright
and not-so-bright. They are as uniquely themselves as
any other human being who walks this earth. No
study has proved why we are Gay or non-Gay. As
parents our hands are clean of causing any sexual or
affectional orientation. We may all wash away our
guilt. Being Gay is a natural condition for those who
are Gay. *Natural.* Homosexuality has always existed

---

*"Gays have typically been somewhat defensive about the butch/femme
stereotype, and for good reason. Both non-Gay feminists and some
Lesbians are opposed to role-taking by Lesbian couples. Non-Gays view
it as a symptom of pathology: some Lesbians view it as a cop-out to
the heterosexist establishment. Gay people should not be judged on
the basis of whether they fit a stereotype. We support the concept of
role flexibility and believe in encouraging individuals to fulfill their
own potential in whatever way seems best to them. We do not
believe, however, that individuals or couples who take butch/femme
roles in all or part of their relationship should be considered 'sick,'
any more than we consider heterosexual couples 'sick' who take these
roles based on gender."

and will continue to exist. It has as much right to exist as any other nondestructive condition of nature.

I give out reprints of a sermon by William Sloane Coffin, Jr., Ph.D., senior minister of the Riverside Church, New York City. Dr. Coffin is nationally recognized for his writing and oratory. I feel that this sermon is responsive to questions previously raised by the parents concerning religion. We leaf through this brilliant clergyman's writing:

> Aside from their extraordinary contributions to human progress and happiness, what did the following have in common: Erasmus, Leonardo da Vinci, Michelangelo, Christopher Marlowe, King James I of England, Sir Francis Bacon, Thomas Gray, Frederic the Great of Germany, Margaret Fuller, Tchaikovsky, Nijinsky, Proust, A. E. Housman, T. E. Lawrence, Walt Whitman, Henry James, Edith Hamilton, W. H. Auden, Willa Cather, and Bill Tilden, the greatest tennis player of all time?
>
> Some of you, no doubt, have the answer. They were all homosexual. . . .

Dr. Coffin goes on to say that he brings up the "once unmentionable" subject of homosexuality because it is "probably the most divisive issue since slavery split the church." He admits that it's difficult for both Gays and straights to approach the subject with "open minds rather than with fixed certainties, with hearts full of compassion rather than repugnance."

So the question is whether those of us who were drilled . . . to think a certain way are as willing as [Peter] to risk re-examining what we were taught. Moral judgment has a progressive character, criticizing the present in terms of the future. Could it be that the Holy Spirit in our time is leading each of us to a new conviction, a new confession: "Truly I perceive that God shows no partiality, but in *every sexual orientation* anyone who fears him and does what is right is acceptable to him...."

Clearly, it is not Scripture that creates hostility to homosexuality, but rather hostility to homosexuality that prompts certain Christians to retain a few passages from an otherwise discarded code...I don't see how Christians can centrally define and then exclude people on the basis of sexual orientation alone—not if the law of love is more important than the laws of biology.

We all agree that this sermon is one of the finest, the fairest and the most logical on the subject of homosexuality by an ecclesiastic that we have read. One father says it is a pity that most ministers, rabbis and priests are not as openminded as Dr. Coffin is, that Dr. Coffin is a truly a man of God.

The father, who has fastened on to the question of "cure," asks again, "Isn't this Gayness treatable?" We refer to Dr. Coffin's sermon:

According to this second view, homosexuals are not criminals or sinners so much as victims of arrested development or some other form of psychic disorder, because fundamentally homosexuality is "unnatural." The problem with this position is that most gay people assert that they did not choose their orientation, they discovered it; and scientific research supports the assertion. Psychology professor John Money, a leading authority on character development, claims that it is not possible to force a change from homosexual to heterosexual "any more than it is possible to change a heterosexual into a homosexual." If that's the case, then the offer to "cure" gays of their sickness carries the danger of raising false expectations, and then guilt when the cure doesn't work.

Dr. Coffin asks if we are willing to risk reexamining what we were taught. "Moral judgment has a progressive character, criticizing the present in terms of the future." He deals with the word *abomination*, which is used in the Bible regarding homosexuality, as well as in connection with eating pork, misusing incense, and having intercourse during menstruation. Generally it does not signify something intrinsically evil (like rape or theft, which are also dealt with in the Levitical code), but something that is "ritually unclean." He notes the distinction between intrinsic wrong and ritual impurity—and who among us has not violated ritual?

Dr. Coffin decries fixed certainties, saying, "If what we think is right and wrong divides still further the human family, there must be something wrong with what we think is right. Enough of this punitive legislation against gay people."

One mother had read Edmund White's *States of Desire: Travels Through Gay America*. Mr. White, a highly regarded Gay writer, has one of his characters say that he does not think we should look to the Bible for answers that had not yet been formulated when it was written. He points out that DNA was unknown in Biblical times; therefore, we would not ask of Scripture answers to complex questions about biology:

In the same way St. Paul never thought in terms of constitutional homosexuality, that is, homosexuality that constitutes the very self of certain individuals. In this day people imagined that homosexuality was a vice that some people chose to adopt and could just as easily abandon.

Since the parents have requested information about local Gay affirmative religious organizations, I read out names and telephone numbers of the following:

- Integrity (Protestant):   (212) 620-0057
- Dignity (Catholic):   (212) 658-5798
- Gay Synagogue (Jewish):   (212) 929-9498
- Metropolitan Community Church: (212) 242-1212

I think some more information on religion is in order for this week's "Philosophical Issues," so I hand out copies of an article by Brian McNaught, "Gay and Catholic" (several members of the group had asked to see this). One of the mothers in the group, a social worker who is devoutly Catholic, seizes with surprise upon certain passages and reads aloud:

"As a Catholic who is also Gay I gamble that the Church has totally misinterpreted the Will and word of God.... The Bible has been used to justify human actions since the first ink dried on Chapter One of Genesis. We have used it to condemn Jews, maintain slaves, keep women in what we imagine to be their 'place,' condemn non-Catholics, condemn borrowing money from banks, condemn masturbation, justify the Crusades, condemn inoculation and a variety of other practices or attitudes we weren't comfortable holding alone but insisted that everyone else hold, too. The Church cites Genesis, Leviticus and Letters of St. Paul to Romans and Corinthians and Timothy to build its case against homosexuality.... There is no arguing with these people except to point out the thousands of violations of the Bible which they commit in a single week... traditions change by the weight of new discovery. Lest anyone be confused, I love the Church."

A woman in the corner speaks up: "What about Judaism?" Anticipating a question about Judaism, I have also brought along several copies of "Judaism in the Gay Community," by Barret L. Brick, who surprises us when we read aloud from *his* article:

"Although the Gay Jewish community as such is barely seven years old, the entire Jewish community is awakening to our voices and is beginning to face the challenge we pose; that we will not longer live a lie to our people. We are both Jewish and Gay; we will not sacrifice one for the other.

"Resolutions of support for Gay rights have already been adopted by the American Jewish Committee, the North American Jewish Students Network, the Philadelphia B'nai B'rith Anti-Defamation League, and Central Conference of American Rabbis, and the Union of American Hebrew Congregations. . . .

"The International Conference of Gay and Lesbian Jews (the word *Lesbian* was added in 1978) is now an annual event. . . .

"It can hardly be denied that Jewish tradition as it developed from at least 2,300 years ago looked upon male homosexual acts of any sort as prohibited in general. . . .

"Procreation, marriage, family life—these imperatives are bound up within Judaism and have continually been cited as prime reasons why homosexuality has no place within Judaism. . . .

"Sexuality within Judaism is not seen as solely procreative in function, but is equally valid as an expression of love in and of itself. If this is the case for non-Gay Jews, this must also be the case for Jews. Once the procreative imperative is removed from sexuality, there is no barrier to a proper understanding of homosexuality within Judaism, save for the centuries-old interpretations of two passages in Leviticus."

After all this affirmative material is presented to the class, Mr. B. stubbornly puts forth again his recurrent quizzical, "But isn't this Gayness treatable?" He harps on this question week after week, like a broken record, and every week Fern temporarily squashes him with a tooth-gnashing, baleful look. It is as though he has walled out what is being said that is positive and leads us to qualify our previous concepts. He does not recognize that there are contrasts—light and shade, not immutability.

Mr. and Mrs. B. and Mr. and Mrs. D. are still clinging to their resistance, even as most of us are beginning to realize that this is not a question of good or bad, sick or well, but of human rights and family solidarity.

I then circulate the following Heterosexual Questionnaire,* which humorously recasts the questions asked of Gay people.

HETEROSEXUAL QUESTIONNAIRE

1. What do you think caused your heterosexuality?

2. When and how did you first decide you were a heterosexual?

3. Is it possible your heterosexuality is just a phase you may grow out of?

*From Martin Rochlin, Ph.D., West Hollywood, CA.

4. Is is possible your heterosexuality stems from a neurotic fear of others of the same sex?

5. If you've never slept with a person of the same sex, is it possible that all you need is a good Gay lover?

6. To whom have you disclosed your heterosexual tendencies? How did you react?

7. Why do you heterosexuals feel compelled to seduce others into your life-style?

8. Why do you insist on flaunting your heterosexuality? Can't you just be what you are and keep it quiet?

9. Would you want your children to be heterosexual, knowing the problems they'd face?

10. A disproportionate majority of child molesters are heterosexuals. Do you consider it safe to expose your children to heterosexual teachers?

11. With all the societal support marriage receives, the divorce rate is spiraling. Why are there so few stable relationships among heterosexuals?

12. Why do heterosexuals place so much emphasis on sex?

13. Considering the menace of overpopulation, how could the human race survive if everyone were heterosexual like you?

14. Could you trust a heterosexual therapist to be objective? Don't you fear (s)he might be inclined to influence you in the direction of her/his own leanings?

15. How can you become a whole person if you limit yourself to compulsive, exclusive heterosexuality,

and fail to develop your natural, healthy homosexual potential?

16. There seem to be very few happy heterosexuals. Techniques have been developed that might enable you to change if you really want to. Have you considered trying aversion therapy?

The parents scan it. Some read it again and again. Two couples mutter that it is presumptuous. One woman smiles:

> "I see. This dishes out to us what we do to them. I suppose that it's we, the straight ones, who are presumptuous. I'm beginning to understand that our assumptions are unjust, but we didn't initiate them, after all. We simply carried on teachings we had received without question until those teachings hit us where we lived. There is so much harm that was done to our children that we must try to undo."

That settled, I then ask the group members to take out paper and pencil and list six questions for their consideration:

1. What was your relationship with your Gay child before disclosure?

2. What is your present relationship?

3. What are your child's admirable qualities?

4. What are your child's less admirable qualities?

5. How would you assess your child as a whole person?

6. What are your hopes for a future relationship?

I tell them I do not plan to see what they write. These questions, however, will lead them into some soul-searching. Faces are screwed up into painful grimaces. When the parents finish writing, I tell them that these questions are a means for each one to learn something about themselves—where they *were*, where they *are* and where they *are going* in their relationships with their Gay children. The discussion that follows confirms that most parents had enjoyed close relationships prior to their new knowledge. Many have listed a new honesty as foremost in their present relationships along with a sense of discovery of the new and different dimensions in their Gay child. Some were doubtful about their relationships before as well as now. Most admit to resistance to revealing their child's homosexuality to family and friends but are now contemplating stratagems as to how and when to deal with this. (They had not faced up to this prior to taking the workshop.)

Although the "admirable qualities" they list and read out aloud vary from person to person, most of the parents praise their children. When it comes to the *less* admirable qualities, the parents complain of "secrecy." (I wonder why!) They also complain of rebellion against the family's standards of behavior, outlandish friends, styles of dress (a common complaint no matter how they are sexually and affectionally oriented).

A sprinkling of parents worry about mannishness in daughters and effeminacy in sons. In general, however, they agree that their children—physicians, psychologists, attorneys, blue- and white-collar workers, artists (hardly ever soldiers, policemen or firemen) have singular talents, roles and characteristics apart from their sexuality.

They all hope that family relationships will not be destroyed by their knowledge. Most of the parents voice the hope that they will be included in their children's lives, sharing in their triumphs and failures. They hope for a fair amount of intimacy, that the children will stay in touch. They want to be able to count on their children when *they* are in need. As frequently as circumstances permit, they want communication.

The few who express doubt about future relationships did say they did not raise these children to lose them because they are Gay and hope that outside pressure will not cause estrangement. By the end of this session, most parents have processed a great deal of new information. We have read and examined the logic of a respected minister, as well as two Gay writers. We have hashed and rehashed the question of the rights of others to pass judgment on our Gay sons and daughters, wondering about the validity of long-standing views that ignore the posture of the American Psychiatric Association.

We have appraised our children before and after they told us about their homosexuality, searchingly and honestly. We try to evaluate their personality traits apart from their homosexuality. We all agree that we are meeting here to learn new ways of understanding. We are thinking hard. The evening ends on a note of contemplation. We look forward to our next-to-last session, when we will hear what our invited guests—our Gay children—have to say.

That night at home I note the reflective ending to the session in my Workshop Journal. Have I thrown too much information at them? Was it too educational and not focused enough on the personal issues that were plaguing them all? From my notebook that night only a short paragraph:

> *By the session's end, most of us have processed what we have learned. We have read and examined the humane logic of a respected cleric, two writers on religious issues, and a questionnaire (which amuses some, irritates others). Have discussed read-*

ings, deliberating over the question of rights of others to pass judgment on Gay kids, wondering about the validity of long-standing views that ignored the decision of the APA. Had appraised our children before and after our new knowledge, searchingly, honestly. Tried to section off their personality traits apart from their Gayness. All agreed we were meeting to learn new ways of understanding. Now we were readying ourselves for the next session to hear what our Gay children had to say.

Week V: The Night the Children Came

The Party was trying to kill the sex instinct or if it could not be killed then to distort it and dirty it. The sex instinct creates a world of its own outside of the party's control and therefore had to be destroyed, if possible.

—George Orwell, *1984*

I scan the room. It is crowded. Everyone has come, including Kenny and Sam. We scurry for more chairs, placing them in concentric circles—the children inside. Gay children. Straight parents. One sister of a Gay brother. Their very presence is a statement that the years of seclusion with their knowledge is over. The room vibrates with anticipation. Silent bells are tolling for a victory over silence. As people find seats, conversation is nervous and animated. The parents had proposed that we invite the children to this meeting so that we could talk about them when we meet for the last session.

I place copies of articles on the table for parents to take home: "The Meaning of Gay"—an interview with C. A. Tripp by Philip Nobile, which had appeared in

New York magazine, and "Overcoming Guilt (A Parent's Defense)" by Ann Muller, which had appeared in *The Advocate*. The parents hang back from taking the article about parents' guilt in front of their kids, but because I find it especially on target, I hawk it: "Anyone for 'Overcoming Guilt'? Try it, you'll like it."

Gingerly, the parents reach for it. The children think this is funny. Expectancy. I welcome our young guests, who range in age from late teens to mid-thirties. They are especially beautiful. I half wish to see at least one exaggerated stereotype present, if only to demonstrate to the parents that they are a minority. One languishing Gay man and one mannish young woman would do. In *Changing Views of Homosexuality*, Elizabeth Ogg notes that

> The Institute for Sex Research estimates that only fifteen percent of male and five percent of female homosexuals are recognizable as such to most people.

Our children are almost uniformly healthy-looking, muscular and exceptionally articulate.

I invite anyone to launch us.

Iris, a young woman who has taken me aside before the session to tell me how shy she is and to ask me to please *not* call on her, jumps right in. A flaxen-haired Brunhilde, Iris begins,

> "I was aware that I was Gay when I was five. I remember managing to break my doll's legs very quickly and shrugging to the family that they 'got broke.' Then I dived for my brother's trucks and trains. I could beat up any boy in my family or in my classes at school. My mother has known that I am Gay for five years. She disapproves. That is why I sent her to this workshop for her birthday. My treat. I'm pretty tough and I don't care what

most people think about me, but my mother *must* love me. Maybe it will happen here."

The eyes of the girl and her mother meet and lock for a long moment.

"I live with another woman. It has been five years for us. When there are small family gatherings, we are invited. But when *everyone* gets together, we are not invited. It hurts."

Her mother counteracts by saying that "there is too much explaining to do" and that she just cannot "hack it."

One man reasons that if this mother has been coming regularly to the workshop, then she is doing something about trying to learn what she can about her daughter's Lesbianism and that perhaps she is declaring her own individuality by taking whatever time she needs to come out to the larger family.

Shelly's daughter Carmen and her lover Tillie are present. There is a fragility about the girl that arouses our protective feelings. Shelly looks the part of downcast mother tonight: resigned, long-suffering. At most other meetings she has been the buoyant spirit. Is she putting on something of an act for her daughter's benefit? Is her usual *apparent* cheerfulness about her daughter and her lover a front to bolster up the other parents? Carmen tells us that she is torn between her mother and her lover. She says there is a rivalry between the two women for her attention and affections.

"I'm always in the middle, trying to placate them. They fuss over me as though I were a baby. I need Tillie. I need my mother. I remember too well how my father treated my mother. We women must stay close. But Mom does not make it easy. My brothers go their own way and do not have to answer to Mom, but I do. And Tillie refuses to tolerate her interference any longer."

All eyes look at Shelly. Accusingly. (When it is someone else's child, we—chameleonlike—become staunch defenders of Lesbian rights.)

Shelly confesses to difficulty in letting go of Carmen and admits that she hopes that their former closeness will continue regardless of Tillie. She wipes her eyes, which have misted over.

"I suppose it was unrealistic of me to believe that she would stay my little girl when she has Tillie. Okay. I surrender you, darling. But I don't want you to go too far away from me. I need you to include me when you can."

Chase, a stocky young man, tells us how pleased he is that his mother has taken this step toward trying to understand his homosexuality by coming to the workshop.

"I am bursting with pride that she has done this for me, but my problem is my older brother. I have been in a group—or maybe I should say a pretty rough gang—with him for the past few years. I have faked being a genuine part of them, of course, but I was afraid not to. Afraid to say that I was Gay and especially afraid to hurt my brother, who would also be put on the spot. My brother would have to defend me against them—*his* friends—or turn against me."

Chase's mother says that she feels that her other son knows about his brother and that Chase should level with him now, before his brother takes a job with the police force, which is his intention.

"I think your brother knows. He just knows. Why don't you have it out with him and then simply ease quietly out of the gang? You don't have to tell those guys if you don't want to, and I do not believe that your brother would tell. It would clear the air at home."

The rest of the group agrees.

A young man, who tells us his name is Jerry, tips his chair back and grins.

"I have to announce that it is *my* mother who no longer drives ten miles to another town to take out library books about Gay life so that our hometown librarian, who is her neighbor, will not know what she is reading. Whatever paranoia she had to deal with about worries that the whole neighborhood would find out what she was reading has really diminished."

His mother Martha says proudly:

"No more looking at my shoes while the books are being stamped and then brown-bagging them as soon as I leave the library. I have nothing to be ashamed of. Rather, I'm proud of myself and less confused about the Gay world now that I am making an open effort to learn something about it."

Martha places her hands on her hips, looking around for approval for what is for her, quite an accomplishment. I distinctly hear a sarcastic, "Well, goody for you" coming from the direction of Mrs. C., but no one else seems to hear it, or at least they ignore it if they do.

Mr. A. tells the young man and his mother that it

is heartening to him to see that this progress is being made and that each time he sees another parent achieve a small victory, his hopes about improving relations with his daughter are getting higher and higher.

The young woman who has been attending our sessions because of concern for her Gay brother proudly introduces Abner.

Abner, a princely looking blond six-footer—(why *are* they all so good-looking or is that a dangerous generalization?)—starts with:

"You have all heard about me. I'm the one who wanted to tell my mother that I'm Gay on Mother's Day, but when my sister brought it before this Board of Directors, I understand that I was vehemently voted down. So I told Dad instead— on Mother's Day. I want to tell Mom on Father's Day. My dad was not surprised and received the news calmly, assuring me that our relationship will continue as warmly as before. However, my sister here is extremely apprehensive about my coming out to our mother. Our parents have been divorced for fifteen years, and the only stable relationship my sister and I could count on was the one we had with each other. The divorce caused us to cling to each other more than most brothers and sisters because we needed to feel that we would not change. Our parents might be split asunder, but we would always be brother and sister.

"Our father has remarried. Our mother has not. She still bears an enormous animosity toward my father, who left her for the woman to whom he is married. Her tolerance for pain and distress is very low. My sister, who has always been my champion, is fearful of seeing any further tearing apart of what's left of the family. She's afraid that my mother will just fall apart if she learns I am Gay."

The sister, now tearful, says, "I just want to safeguard some family unity. Why does he feel he has to tell her?"

One of the young Gay guests remarks that she would feel stifled if she could not face her mother with the truth about herself. Another young man says that Abner should take the plunge and trust in his mother that she would come through for him. Some parents say, "Wait"; others ask, "Wait for what?"

Nothing is settled except that both brother and sister express relief and gratitude that here is a place where they can air their problem in the presence of sympathetic people. They will take the problem home and think about it, weighing what they have heard at the session.

I remark that the onset of widespread divorce has thrown many siblings into a symbiosis that might not have otherwise occurred had the family remained intact. The fact of one sibling's homosexuality pales in importance, next to the crumbling of parental ties. And so the brothers and sisters hold tightly to each other as the only solidly remaining family they have. Abner's sister does not want his being Gay to rock what is left of the boat.

A young Hispanic Gay man tells us that his mother's acceptance means the world to him.

"Sometimes we Spanish say that you always know who your mother is, but you can't ever be sure about your father. I think that's true. When I read all the articles my mother brings home from the workshop, it gives me hope for our getting together. She's stopped crying about my being Gay and has invited my lover for dinner for the first time. He and I will cook because she's such a terrible cook. But it's nice to have my mother back again talking to me and looking at me with the same pleasure I saw in her eyes before she knew."

The parents appear to be quite comfortable with the Gay contingent, absorbed in every word that they share with us.

Zed, one of the young men present, almost knocks us out with what he has to say.

"My mother called me up last week to ask me if I would impregnate the Lesbian daughter of her best friend. This daughter had told her mother that she had every intention of getting pregnant either by artifical insemination, which, as we all have probably heard or read, is becoming more and more *au courant* with Lesbian women, or by a handpicked, willing guy. The mother was panicky, thinking that the donor, or stud, might be any kind of two-headed freak and, using my mother as a go-between, suggested that I do the good deed because she 'knows my background.'"

Zed's mother becomes defensive: "Well, Zed, it would have been one way for me to become a grandma."

The group's interest is piqued. They clamor to know what Zed had said. Zed, a physician, is serene.

"I said that if the girl would take fertility pills, give birth to twins and give me one, then I would think about it. But no way would I father a child to give up."

Zed's mother is angry.

"I told my son that these are *children* we are talking about. Not kittens. To forget I ever mentioned it. Anyway, suppose she had triplets?"

I note that some of the parents are addressing hypothetical questions to Sam and Kenny, probably tapping in to them because of their respective professions and the degree of peace they have made with their respective families. However, apart from convivial interchange, the Gay children did not join in this interrogation, most of them having been already well doctored by their own therapists and secure in their self-knowledge.

A few of the children are intent on placing their parents in the hot seat; some are turning over why they themselves were in or out of the closet at work or socially. But most have come to the session to validate their hopes for improved relations with their families.

Wilma's son talks at length about the needs of Gay offspring not to lose touch with their parents—not to be judged solely for being Gay.

"Since I have moved in with my father, I find that my relationship with my mother and stepfather is much better. Maybe I had to go away to come back. My stepfather and I have long talks about what it was like for me—growing up Gay in secret— and we are developing a real friendship. My mother and I are finally talking nonstop. It's great."

Mr. and Mrs. H. look fondly, but worriedly, at their pretty and vivacious daughter Delia, who is accompanied by a lovely young woman. Delia speaks eloquently about herself:

"I took the coming out step six months ago, telling my parents I was Gay at about the same time I was accepted into a doctoral program at a local university. I suppose I needed to celebrate my acceptance with my parents' eyes opened about me. I needed them to really see me—inside, not just outside. Like where did I get my blue eyes or who in the family did I take after? What I looked like *inside*. As you know, my folks are typically Italian-American. The closely knit family is all—and let no one drop a stitch.

"My father is doing a fair amount of soul-searching these days, wondering what went amiss with me and peering far down into the old traditions and attitudes that he now admits were certainly put-downs of women. No matter how I try to reassure him that it was not the macho Italian outlook that turned me Lesbian and off men, he insists on putting blame there. Although he is reading books from your list and the articles you gave out, he is still not convinced entirely that he was not at the root of my being Gay.

"My mother is still hugging her hurt to her breast. But her agitation has decreased since she has been coming to these meetings. Not only because I love my parents with all my heart and always will but because I must, of economic necessity, live at home for the next two years, is it so important to me that they take me as I really am—Gay. I need to be taken into their hearts without holding back. I know I am asking the moon, but I love this girl [*gesturing toward her companion*] and I want to be able to see her freely in the home I make with my parents. I have a younger sister. My mother forbids me to tell her I am Gay. This cuts me up, but, as I said, I'm

Italian. I will obey my mother and wait for her to say when."

Kenny takes issue with that. He throws his challenge at her. Why does she need to be controlled by her parents at *her* age? After all, she is not a minor.

James flares up. "It's called filial respect, young man."

I interrupt to say that this is not a therapy session as much as a coming together on common ground for the families of Gay people. These children are our guests. We are not here to uncover what makes us tick, but to look perhaps at the sociology that has so divided us and to try to bridge the resulting gaps. And to listen to what our children say. Really listen to them.

Delia continues, "I have every intention of having children one day. I love children. I am going to be a good mother."

Obviously this is a pronouncement her parents have not heard before. Their shock shows on their faces. Still, Delia has the floor:

"I do not believe that women should indulge in casual sex. I do not believe that a woman under the age of eighteen should experiment sexually. There is nothing more intimate than the act of love and it should be reserved for those one really feels for when one is old enough to know what one is doing. And when one is committed—it should be forever."

Delia rests her case. Very positive. Defiant. We are all speechless. I might have been listening to one of my Philadelphia school marms of the forties. This young woman is following the lead of her heterosexual parents to a tee, except that she has someone of the same sex in mind.

James poses a question to the group: How long have they known they were Gay? A Greek chorus answers, "Oh, very long. Probably always." Numbers upward from five, seven, eight years old startle us.

Wilma, teary-eyed again, whispers, "And you were alone for so long with this knowledge?"

Another young woman, who happens to be a funeral director, closes our session. She decries the embarrassment her father is made to feel at anti-Gay remarks, the unfeelingness and hostility of society, and calls for unity of spirit from the families with their Gay children.

The evening ends on a note of exhilaration. Of hope for better things to come. Certainly it is a first for Kenny and Sam, who, although they are veterans of many group counseling sessions, had not experienced a confrontation such as this.

Brick is effusive. He says that he has grown astronomically. I grin, feeling good about myself. I almost kiss my shoulder.

I watch the children leave with their parents. They are talking excitedly. They have never before experienced such an evening. Many of them earn more money than their parents. They do not need us for financial support anymore. They need us for a different kind of support.

Will we be there?

Much later I write in my Workbook Journal after a dinner at an elegant Chinese restaurant with Kenny and Sam:

Reviewed evening with Kenny and Sam. Both agree that they are intrigued and excited by the workshop. Sam observes that most of the group really listen. Kenny notes look of pride most parents bestow on their offspring when child has floor and general reaction of attractiveness and intelligence of the Gay sons and daughters. Impressed with rise and fall of mood. How we swing from serious breast-beating to good-humored banter. Do so many sessions end on high note because we are able to relieve tension by laughing at ourselves? Sam recalls all-around handshakes of good night, murmurs of "Glad to have been here, hope it happens soon again." Kenny, Sam and I hoped such scenes would be repeated—many times, many places.

For next week's last session bring list of professional organizations for Gay men and Lesbians to keep group upbeat when they're on their own.

Week VI: The Last Meeting

Although I place copies of "A Disturbed Peace" (Brian McNaught) and "What Homosexuals Want" (Letitia Anne Peplau) around the table, the group is feeling too festive to read about other Gay kids. I notice the material is tucked away in handbags and pockets to be read later—not tonight.

They have thought of everything: assorted cheeses, jug wines, Cheese Doodles, apples and grapes. We are all starting to feel very loose. One woman has even baked a kugel. People like each other here. And, of course, we have our slightly unusual common bond: our Gay children.

Brick wants to know when our next reunion will be. I remind him that this is not camp. We are meeting here with a serious mission in mind and we should try to remember what it is.

Mrs. A. says that this workshop was just the tip of the iceberg. Why don't we as the "advanced" group continue to meet once a week at the Y on a different night? I regard the group, palms up, questioning? Yes! was the consensus. Enthusiastically, yes!

We decide to meet in the fall and spring once a week for six weeks at the Y. I make a note to put the evening aside.

Shelly says that there will surely be new issues cropping up with a Gay family member in our midst and that we are sure to need each other for support to deal with them. Wilma agrees, thinking aloud about a number of family celebrations coming up in the fall.

"We have not yet unveiled our son to our extended family. He is sure to want to bring his—uh, buddy. I am going to have plenty to discuss with you all in the fall about how I manage or mismanage his debut."

Fern is taking names and addresses. She is actually forming a parent support group. They will feel free to call each other in the event of crisis somewhat in the manner of AA or Overeaters Anonymous.

I ask the group what they feel had been accomplished by the participation of our Gay children. Brick says:

"In listening to them I see now that the meaningfulness of our lives rests on our shoulders—not our children's."

Fern says:

"I felt that the free flow of questions and the talk was so liberating. I never would have thought to discuss those things with my son years ago. When I next see him, I am going to probe as much as he will allow me. What I once thought was an invasion of privacy is actually a show of interest—of caring and concern for him."

Wilma says:

"I have advanced through listening to them so that I externalize more. I have really heard about the pain they felt and I carry guilt for not being aware of it all these years where my own son was concerned. I want to make up for the aloneness that he felt. That *now* I am walking with him."

James says:

"I saw with tremendous admiration the strides most of the young women who talked with us have made in their careers and listened to the plans the others have for their future success. I admit that I saw my daughter's Lesbianism as a denial of me. That in rejecting men, she rejected me. But after all the readings and discussions, I am convinced that her being Gay is happenstance. I hope that she will advance as far as her brother, but if she does not, she has my love and support, anyway. We are getting to know each other in a different way. Every time we meet I have a sense of discovery about this young woman—this daughter of mine."

Mr. A.:

"It was getting through to me finally that my wife and I had better rechart our expectations of our daughter. That she is a healthy, productive young woman and is not here to enhance our expectations of her. Kenny, Sam and the other young people present came across loud and clear that they wished with all their hearts to preserve family unity but not at the too-dear cost of denying who they were."

Mr. B.:

"My wife and Mr. and Mrs. C. still feel that the kids' visit here does not solve anything. We want to know if being Gay can be detected early? If so, can it be arrested?

Fern (snorting):

"Arrested?"

Mr. D.:

"Perhaps scientists will discover a means of ferreting out Gay kids early on and maybe redirect it. They would be like everyone else and our problems would be gone."

Brick expostulates:

"Sure, let's create a world of clones. Nature makes over twenty million of them different, hurting no one, and we are going to 'arrest' them. I like your choice of verb. What did you have in mind— 'straightening-out lobotomies'?"

The B.'s, D.'s and Brick bristle at each other. I speak up:

"Peace. Hey, *Shalom*. This is a winding-up-the-end celebration. Please remember that this workshop is based on our true perceptions of our Gay children. We are dealing with independent beings. We are not here to hypothesize why and how, but to face what is. These extraordinary children cared enough about our love and acceptance to attend the session. Their very presence speaks volumes as to their need to perpetuate family relationships. Not to be told that we must concentrate on dissecting the potentially Gay so that their very existence would become extinct. I consider such tampering to be against nature. Against God, if you will."

Mr. G.:

"My daughter was glad to have been at the session, but she thought the men took over a bit much. But that's par for the course. She says they always take the reins, and when she resists this, it gets sticky. She resented the way we plied Ken and Sam with questions, but we reminded her that lots of people do this when they meet doctors. Brain-drain, I mean. And that it was helpful to us. It was the first time I heard answers from professional Gay people that I could live with."

Mr. H.:

"I'm resigned, but my wife is not. She still feels that our daughter is going through a stage and that is why she doesn't want her to tell her younger sister. Actually, my wife thinks that, but she knows deep down that this is no stage. We were both dumbfounded when our daughter said that someday we would become grandparents and that there would be no son-in-law in the picture. We have not digested her supposed Lesbianism yet. I think she went off half-cocked to talk about getting pregnant at this time in all of our lives. Selfish. Inconsiderate. She had no business doing that last week. We are certainly entitled to more time to get used to the idea of her and this girl she sees. Much more time."

Mr. E.:

"Look. I don't like to wear the monkey suit required for the work I do. But I wear it. I would prefer jeans. That is the conformity we live by in this society if we are going to make it. My son talked about feeling free to exhibit himself as Gay. But we—none of us—are really free. We all have to answer to someone. Even the President answers to Congress. I understand my son's resentment about living underground. And I appreciate that he showed up for the session. It did him good. It did me good. But I argue that he must be very selective and discreet in his line of work especially. He does not know what it is not to have a paycheck. I have lived through the Depression. I implore him to keep his mouth shut. I hope he listens."

I say:

"I believe that your son's own inner comfort comes first. Maybe he cannot live with your fears. He has to decide for himself. He is an adult with the right to take risks if he chooses. You must keep your fears away from him. Let go."

Brick (howling):

"I do feel better about my kid until I think about her being in bed with that other *girl!*"

I say:

"Brick, you have been in and out of crisis therapy. Do you think it would help if you saw your therapist on this 'bed' issue and explored your feelings about it?"

Brick subsides somewhat but agrees that he will give his therapist a call. I look at my watch.

"It is seven-thirty. Curtain time for this workshop until the fall. Would you like to sum up what you feel you have learned here to change your outlook? Or not learned?"

Some of the remarks from different members of the workshop:

"I am finally relying on the strength of my husband and my close friends. In doing so I have come to realize how I was programmed to reject the very idea of homosexuality, which embodies my own child."

"I am contending with my own personal closet. I am not militant or strident, but my psychological health has improved. I don't feel tied up in knots anymore."

"I have wasted so much positive energy deploring my Gay child. I am determined to turn that wasted energy around and enrich my life by getting to know just *who* my child really is."

There are those whose lips are still set in thin lines. But just a few. All told, there is the feeling of having been on a singular adventure. We raise our

Styrofoam cups as Brick toasts, "Here's to whatever we tell our friends and relatives. Gulp."

I make a little speech:

> "I am passing out a three-part questionnaire. You may sign it or not. Please mail it back or phone it in. Remarks are welcome. I need to know what changes, if any, this workshop has caused in you, in your attitude about your Gay children and the validity of this kind of a workshop. I would also like to know if you find that you have added strengths to face other life issues since you have taken on this big one head-on.
>
> "If this workshop has been something of a catalyst in helping you deal with the concepts that were set in your minds in concrete, I am grateful that you have allowed it to work. If not, but you have struck down some of those graven images and moved forward even a little bit to clasp your Gay child close, I am grateful. Coming out for parents is as ongoing as it is for their Gay children.
>
> "But if all failed and you are like the Sphinx—immovable—then I am sorry. Sorry to know that inevitably your Gay children will remove themselves from you. And it will be a terrible loss."

We gather around kissing good-bye and wishing each other a healthy, happy summer. There is almost a family feeling.

From the corner of one eye, I notice James and one of the single women departing arm-in-arm. They are smiling broadly at each other. Romance? My God. They each have two Gay kids. Has research been done yet on heterosexual marriages that include a bevy of Gay stepchildren?

Later at home I summarized our progress in my Workshop Journal—it was not to be the last entry. There are more, I hope, to come.

Wilma says not one person in group she would not have liked for a friend, that we were all different but the common bond of Gay children was so important. Says she thought our Gay children lucky to have us as parents! General enthusiasm about meeting once a week at the Y in the fall. Most feel need of ongoing support group. Decided to call on each other for help over the summer if need be. Most parents braced for inevitable trials and tribulations ahead now that their children are out of closet—within and outside family. Some steadfast in feeling more prudent for entire family to remain closeted. Three-part questionnaire to be mailed back to me or telephoned in.

    Conclusion: Although we are at different stages of reaction, general agreement that we are bound and determined to make healthy adaptation to Gay children. Great workshop!

The concept of ongoing workshops for families of Gay people, professionally led, size-limited and meeting weekly for six sessions at a community organization is in the embryonic stage at this time. It is my hope that in the near future this will change: that the helping institutions in cities small, mid-sized and large will take the cue from what is being offered in some New York area Y's. But until the dawn of that happy time, parents of Gay children who do not have access to such workshops may take heart that they are not alone. Some of us are doing something to rescue our relationships with our Gay children.

QUESTIONNAIRE

I asked the parents to answer the following questions and return the questionnaire to me at home:

1. How has this workshop affected your relationship with your Gay child or children?

2. How has this workshop affected your personal feelings toward your Gay child or children?

3. Do you feel differently about the subject of homosexuality since attending the workshop? If so, how?

Epilogue

Some months after I had graduated from Fordham, I joined Ortho, a professional organization that has an interdisciplinary approach to mental health—and a prestigious membership of thousands. Traditionally they send out a call for abstracts summarizing ideas for workshops to be considered for their annual conferences about a year in advance. I received an application for the 61st Annual Meeting to be held in Toronto in April 1984. Here was my opportunity—to suggest a workshop on a family in crisis when a child is discovered to be Gay.

I examined the application gingerly. I was such a recent graduate. Should I try? Would my abstract be considered? How could I compete with other professionals who had been in practice for ages? Where had I been for so many years that I blossomed at this late date?

Since I often conferred with Kenny—now a clinical psychologist with a successful practice of his own—about the problems of clients I counseled, I called him that night to discuss both a client and the Ortho abstract. When I told him about Ortho, Kenny said, "Sure, go for it." The concerns of families of Gay people were too long a neglected area. A workshop at Ortho was needed, we agreed. I asked Kenny, "Will you join me in Toronto if they take it?"

"We'll see."

I received a call one fall day from Ortho advising me that the workshop, "My Child is Homosexual: A Family Crisis," was scheduled. I would be the moderator and was Dr. Morgen joining me?

I called Kenny, breathless. Pitiless and exasperated, he said, "Mom, I'd rather you did this yourself. I have no interest in becoming the Gay poster boy of the year or in seeing Mommy/Kenny dolls on the market. Remember parent/child separation-individuation? This is something you can do very well on your own."

I blanched. No, I couldn't! How could I, brandnew social worker that I was, present before my peers at a professional meeting? I called Ortho to bow out. I spoke to Dr. Judith Platt, who interrupted with, "Wait. Don't panic. Call Emery Hetrick." Emery, the eminent Gay psychiatrist who is so active in the concerns of Gay youth and their families.

I did call Emery and he agreed to take over the workshop. I would be on the panel. He included other panelists, among them Rose Robertson, an English social worker who founded Parents' Enquiry, an organization in England dedicated to serve the needs of Gay people and their families.

As it turned out, the much needed workshop went well and was enthusiastically received. And it was there that I met Rose.

Rose Robertson,* my English counterpart, is light-

*Rose and I socialized while in Toronto at the Ortho meeting. What I say of her is compounded of what she said at the panel discussion, what she told Gene and me and what she said during our interview.

years ahead of me in achievement and knowledge. The daughter of a British Naval officer, Rose was raised to be stalwart and sturdy in the old tradition of the United Kingdom. She recalls hanging on to her father's neck when she was only two years old while he dove from the high board into the water. That is how she learned to swim—and perhaps how to swim in life's deeper waters.

This white-haired, ultramarine-eyed social worker founded Parents' Enquiry, and agency that serves some of the needs of the families of Gay people, and especially Gay youngsters. The Greater London Council is supportive of the agency, which has come to be known and respected throughout the United Kingdom.

Like me, Rose has two sons—one Gay and one non-Gay.

Unlike me, Rose dreamed of and saw come to fruition the formation of an agency concerned with familial Gay issues and is government-approved. The agency often trains social work students to counsel these families fairly and without bias, as part of their internship.

It was not easy for her, of course.

Rose went through her own personal trial by fire in her struggle to understand and come to terms with her son's homosexuality. Rose told of how her son revealed his homosexuality to her.

"My reaction was one of disbelief. In 1966 it was illegal to be Gay. In 1967 the Sexual Law Reform Act made it legal for men of the age of twenty-one to be practicing homosexuals. That is, behind *locked*—not closed—doors.

"I had always been interested in the problems of young people in my work. Now I had to face the problems of the young in the bosom of my own family. I rejected myself. This could not happen to people like me. Stages of anger smoldered through me as I realized that society could say that my son did not exist, that this loving human being who wants to love and give love could be jailed. It was barbaric.

"After about one year, my anger turned outward. I looked around as a social worker at the other Gay youngsters in similar situations. It appeared that most of them could not tell their parents. Then I switched my professional interest to them and to their parents."

Rose opened her home to her Gay son's friends, too. These young people made her more alert to and aware of their predicament. Her non-Gay son maintained his warm relationship with his brother, often kidding him about how lucky he was not to have the female problems that beset straight men. Her husband remained as he was—"one of the kindliest people I have ever known with no conception of evil. He was very supportive." (Rose's husband died in the spring of 1984.)

Rose remembered how in the early months of her new knowledge there were hurtful and angry exchanges between her son and her. She felt an utter failure. She felt raw and open to any anti-Gay remark, but also fiercely protective, even using that protectiveness against her child.

Rose searched the literature for the flaws in medical and psychological research.

"Nothing I read seemed to have any relation to the little human being I watched grow up. He was not a clinical study. He was my son."

She thought about the reported percentages of homosexual people.

"If those numbers are even close, then thousands of mothers and fathers must be going through absolute hell.

"That closet feeling is so isolating. It must reflect on the child. The fear of what other people might think. Would they think one too clever or not clever enough? The conspiracy of silence."

Rose believes that most Gay men prefer to have a lasting relationship, but that they come so late to a self-accepting self-realization that they mature later: thus, the "hopping around." She sees men as basically hunters—biologically different emotionally and physically from women. More predatory. But, says Rose, she feels that women—both Lesbian and straight—look for emotional security and roots.

"This affects us as parents in that when we see our Gay children—that is, Gay sons—with a succession of lovers, we tend to believe that rapid turnover is the nature of Gay men. Men do hunt. Men who love men compound the hunting instinct."

But Rose believes that this does pass and that eventually Gay men want to settle down. I see Rose Robertson as a dauntless original—a foot solider!

I heard what went unsaid when she discussed her early efforts to establish Parents' Enquiry. Rose could hardly have been cheered on by the society around her. She must have climbed hills if not mountains of protests.

Rose and I—although working on opposite sides of the Atlantic, had a common bond: that of social workers bent on leading families of Gay people toward deeper understanding and acceptance of their Gay children. Although our goal is less than popular, we—and I hope the readers of this book—will see some progress toward it in our lifetime.

More Information

SO YOU'RE TELLING THE FOLKS!

Mom, guess what!
Dad, guess what!

I do not have the count, but many parents have confided in me that one or both had already suspected that their child was Gay. If your homosexuality has been unspoken between you, but *you* need to bring it out in the open, then do it with caution. Use your own judgment.

1. Take the chance
If you have a reasonably upbeat and positive relationship with one or both of your parents, take a deep breath and plunge when you are good and ready. Chances are that after their initial shock—and hurt—your parents will come through for you as they always have. Given time. These are not the olden days but the eighties: the days of *La Cage aux Folles* and *Torch Song Trilogy*. Very likely because of

this, your parents will be more well-read and informed about the subject than they would have been even five years ago.

2. **Think twice**

   If your relationship with one or both of your parents has been on shaky ground, think about whether coming out will exacerbate this already weak relationship. Will it make it well? Better? Be honest *first* with *yourself!* Role-play your mother or father or both.

3. **Consider important questions before you bring up the subject**

   Are your parents in a good marriage or not? Would you be used as a pawn if their marriage is in trouble? Is one parent recently widowed? Are your parents embroiled in personal trauma—tax problems, legalities, adulteries, in-law problems, problems with other siblings, or illnesses? Are they so intensely religious that the idea of your being Gay would be unthinkable to countenance? If any of the above situations is present, perhaps it is *not* the time to come out. You might be ready—but are your parents? It might be prudent to wait until the time is ripe for *them*.

4. **Try coming out to a trusted other relative first**

   You might tell a brother, sister, aunt, uncle, grandparent or cousin before you tell your parents. Test the waters.

5. **Do not come out on special occasions**

   Don't come out on Mother's Day (to Mom), Father's Day (to Dad), Yom Kippur, Christmas Day (or Eve), parents' anniversary, Dad's birthday or Mom's birthday. Rather, after dinner—perhaps with a drink in hand on a weekend when you—and they—are rested and relaxed. Gently does it. Timing is everything in life.

6. **Don't be disappointed if they greet your revelation with shock and hurt**
Give them time to assimilate the news. Even if it seems now that you have known about yourself practically forever, remember how it really took you a long time to come to terms with your sexuality. Be patient with them. If they read you the riot act, lose their speech temporarily, or need to proceed haltingly at their own pace until they arrive at point one where they will then have to begin again with you as a Gay person instead of the straight child they thought they knew, allow for this. They have rights, too.

7. **Help them cope**

- Put them on the mailing lists of Gay affirmative organizations.

- Help them puncture the anti-Gay myths by telling them about eminent, successful and productive Gay people.

- Suggest Gay affirmative books (see pages 235–236).

- Tell them about Parents of Gays and Lesbian groups in their locale.

- Put them in contact with other parents of Gay people who have come to terms (Gay friends' parents, for example).

- Clip out and show them news items of gross unfairness toward Gay people, which should raise their consciousness.

- Keep the lines of communication open.

- Let your hair down—tell them how it was for you—the burden (and now the unburdening).

- Introduce them to your Gay friends.

They will gradually get used to the you that really is—but it takes work—on your part as well as theirs.

WHAT'S A PARENT TO DO?

"From what I have seen the harm to a homosexual man or woman done by the person's trying to convert is multifold. Homosexuals should be warned. First of all, the venture is almost certain to fail."

—Dr. George Weinberg
Society and the Healthy Homosexual

Dr. Weinberg's statement is advocated by many competent professionals, and from my own observations I most assuredly agree. For the parent who accepts the fact that a son or daughter's homosexuality does not go away like the common cold, here are suggestions for restructuring and keeping your relationship with your adult Gay son or daughter intact.

1. **Protest**
   With your *vote*. (You hurt my kid, you hurt me!) You can counteract the politicos who try to deny your Gay child rights. Families have muscle. Millions are family to a Gay person. *Protest* by writing to anti-Gay newspapers about their unjust attitudes and to those advertisers who sponser rabid anti-Gay speakers on radio or television thundering that oppressive action be taken against your Gay children. Write to

advertisers who sponsor programs that forever depict Gay people as losers. (For example, CBS's *Ellis Island* wherein the Lesbian portrayed by Kate Burton and her lover *had* to die via suicide and murder.) Just once, if only to break that relentless pattern, suggest in your letters that it would be novel and refreshing to see a heroic Gay person. (In real life they *do* exist.) Don't buy their soap till they clean up their act. Write to compliment advertisers who show a Gay person as fine and understanding (as in ABC's *Consenting Adult*).

2. **Be accepting**
   Accept what you cannot change. If you loved your Gay child yesterday, remember that this is the same child only with new and different dimensions today.

3. **Flex your own psychic muscles:**
   Rejoice that you are about to widen your world and get to know another side of your child as well.

4. **Question**
   We in the United States are privileged to be able to challenge old precepts. So, how valid are those past Biblical, philosophical and cultural dogmatic teachings if they effect the exclusion of your Gay child? Should they not be modified in accordance with present-day knowledge and thinking? Homosexuality is only one of the many no-nos dictated in past teachings. Many homophobics have chosen to concentrate on homosexuality while disregarding many other proscribed acts such as abortion, divorce, dietary laws, adultery and free love. Are there any of us who can say that he or she has followed dogma to the letter?

5. **Continue to have high expectations for your child**
   Know that your Gay son or daughter may achieve success and happiness despite many still-existing barriers. Although it is acknowledged that one of

the greatest military leaders of all time—Alexander the Great—was a homosexual, a career in the military is not now available to an openly Gay person. What is the military afraid of?

Need I point out the many successful Gay people who have reached the top? If your child is in a profession, say dentistry, he or she can create smiles as chicolety as the non-Gay dentist. If in medicine, perhaps your child will come up with a cure for cancer. If in the right place at the right time, your child might save the life of the President of the United States by grabbing the arm of a crazed would-be assassin as an unofficially Gay war veteran did some years ago in San Francisco.

6. **Don't dwell too much on the sexual aspects of homosexuality**
Don't peer too closely into the bedroom of a Gay son or daughter—you wouldn't with a straight child, would you? Sexual privacy is their right—just as yours is your right. If, however, the Gay child insists on drawing you unwillingly into personal sexual discussion, you have every right to protest: "Spare me the details—and did you remember to send your grandfather a birthday card?"

7. **Learn to enjoy Gay culture**
When given free rein, many Gay people have a special sense of fun and the ridiculous. Even if their humor is a defense (as some say), it is a valuable defense. Relax with the two-sided humor of your Gay child. You might enjoy a lot of laughs together.

8. **Redefine the word** *family*
Today we have new definitions of the word *family*. Among them: the one-parent family, the communal family and same-sex couples. The chimerical *Saturday Evening Post* representation of Dad, Mom

and the two kids smiling into the sunrise just does not hold true anymore. The families of Gay people who want to relate comfortably to their Gay children must face the reality that the paired-off male and female children have what most of us hope for: a shared life with a loving partner. How long a relationship will last—or how fulfilling it might be—is anyone's guess. Gay relationships are just as chancy as non-Gay relationships (and we all know how chancy they are).

9. **Respect your Gay son or daughter**
Remember the respect you had for this child before the disclosure. You have been entrusted with as in-depth a revelation as you will ever get from anyone. This mutuality of respect must not be diminished. It is too precious. Of course, if there was no prior respect, it will not suddenly materialize after disclosure.

10. **Look to your future**
If you are already old and gray, divorced or widowed, this admonition still applies. That is, that either you or your spouse will go first and that the lone survivor will reap the benefits or the barrenness of whatever was planted in your attitude toward your Gay children. If you have invested the love and the efforts that most of us would like to believe that we have invested in our children, you would hope to see a return on that investment in the shape of contact and caring in later years. But if children are made to feel unloved and unworthy by parents because of a condition of being over which they have no control, they usually remove themselves from the parents, causing them pain both physically and emotionally.

Then when the time of your need arrives, that reviled Gay child may be out of reach. Fortunately, many people mellow about past fought-over beliefs as they age. They look around to see who is there for them. The sexuality of those near and dear becomes meaningless. People become simply people—loving or unloving, tender or not, considerate or inconsiderate. The older person has seen so much: life, death, birth. The focus is on what they have now, and life may be enriched by the children involved in it, Gay or non-Gay.

11. Tell others just how much you feel comfortable with

When you are pushed to the wall and feel that evasions are beneath your dignity and, just as importantly, beneath the dignity of your Gay son or daughter, you may say, "This is his (her) friend; this is the person with whom he (she) lives; this is my child's life-style." Then drop it or go on to discuss your child's merits. It goes back to my former statement about having respect for your offspring and the beneficial results of that respect.

12. Join or start a Parents of Gays support group

Assuming that you are a traditional type of person who was brought up with the rights and wrongs of yesteryear, and have done your share of eyebrow raising at the unconventionality of others, now you are in the same position to have eyebrows raised at you.

It hurts.

I know it hurts.

You do not have to be phony. You do not have to pretend to be comfortable with this if you are not. If you say, "Yes, she is a Lesbian, but I'm not happy about it, I'm still working on it," you are on the road to desensitization. You are talking honestly. It gets easier with time.

If you are not asked a direct question, you do not have to answer; you may say whatever makes you comfortable.

If you are asked a direct question, you may deflect it, saying, "Ask him yourself."

There is no need to be defensive.

You have choices.

There are those with whom you would never discuss anything at issue, including your child's sexuality—so don't.

If you think that friends will desert you, let them desert you. This is a time to find out if they were really friends after all.

As you become more used to the idea of having a Gay child (and you must help yourself along), you will probably find yourself so desensitized that your replies to questions will be rote.

It might someday go like this at the bridge table.

"So when is Barbara getting married?"

"Probably never. She's a Lesbian. Two spades."

"Two no trump."

And the game goes on.

Bibliography

Borhek, M. V. *Coming Out to Parents, A Two-Way Survival Guide for Lesbians and Gay Men and Their Parents.* New York: Pilgrim Press, 1983.

Brown, H. *Familiar Faces, Hidden Lives.* New York: Harcourt Brace Jovanovich, 1976.

Carlson, H. M. "Some Information for Parents and Families of Lesbians and Gays, 1984." Available from the Office of Social and Ethical Responsibility for Psychology, American Psychological Association, 1200 Seventeenth Street N.W. Washington, DC 20036.

Clarke, D. *Loving Someone Gay.* Meilbrae, California: Celestial Arts, 1977.

Fricke, Aaron. *Reflections of a Rock Lobster: A Story About Growing Up Gay.* Boston, Massachusetts: Alyson Publications, 1981.

Hobson, Laura Z. *Consenting Adult.* New York: Warner Books, Inc., 1976.

Jones, Clinton R. *Understanding Gay Relatives and Friends.* New York: Seabury Press, 1978.

Reid, John. *The Best Little Boy in the World*. New York: Putnam, 1973.

Russo, Vito. *The Celluloid Closet*. New York: Harper & Row, 1981.

Scanzoni, L. and Mullenkott, V. *Is the Homosexual My Neighbor?* New York: Harper & Row, 1978.

Silverstein, Charles. *A Family Matter*. New York: McGraw-Hill, 1978.

Weinberg, George. *Society and the Healthy Homosexual*. New York: St. Martin's Press, 1972.

Weitzman, Marcia. *Homosexuality as Viewed from Five Perspectives*. Washington, DC: NF/PFG Library Service, 1984.

Catalogs may be ordered from the following Gay affirmative bookstores:

Lambda Rising, 2012 S Street, N.W. Washington, DC 20009 (800) 621–6969.

Oscar Wilde Memorial Bookshop, 15 Christopher Street, New York, New York 10014 (212) 255–8097.

A Different Light, 548 Hudson Street, New York, New York 10014 (212) 989-4850 or 4014 Santa Monica Boulevard, Hollywood, California 90029 (213) 668-0629.

For resource and library materials contact:

NF/PFG *Library Service*, 5715 16th Street, N.W. Washington, DC 20011 (202) 726–3223.

National Gay Task Force, 80 Fifth Avenue, Suite 1601, New York, New York 10011 (212) 741–5800.

Parents FLAG, Box 24565, Los Angeles, California 90024 (213) 472–8952.